3 0132 0085⬛ ✦ KV-639-101

JRS

THE TREASURE CHEST

Out of the blue, Carol Trevallan had been contacted by a firm of solicitors in Falmouth, Cornwall. They had asked her to go down to see them in order to discuss something that would be to her advantage. On the train, Carol meets an American called Mark, and finds herself becoming attracted to him. But when she walks into an old curio shop and comes face to face with Seth Coombes, Carol feels a sense of belonging . . .

Books by Catherine Riddell
in the Linford Romance Library:

TROPICAL DREAMS

CATHERINE RIDDELL

THE TREASURE CHEST

Complete and Unabridged

LINFORD
Leicester

First published in Great Britain in 1998

First Linford Edition
published 2003

British Library CIP Data

Riddell, Catherine
    The treasure chest.—Large print ed.—
Linford romance library
    1. Love stories
    2. Large type books
    I. Title
    823.9'2 [F]

ISBN 0–7089–4930–4

Published by
F. A. Thorpe (Publishing)
Anstey, Leicestershire

Set by Words & Graphics Ltd.
Anstey, Leicestershire
Printed and bound in Great Britain by
T. J. International Ltd., Padstow, Cornwall

This book is printed on acid-free paper

1

After a cursory glance at the single sheet of paper, Carol screwed the letter and its envelope into a ball, took careful aim at the wastepaper basket and promptly missed! Snorting at her miserable failure, she snatched her shoulder bag from the chair and went to the door, glancing in the mirror on the way.

Wide brown eyes peered back at her in a face that some would describe as attractive, pretty even, though Carol would never agree with anyone who said so. Ever conscious of her large eyes, she laughingly said they made her seem as if she was in a state of constant surprise, wondering how anyone could see them as appealing.

Pausing long enough to apply her lipstick, she groaned at the lips she despaired of — full and pouting, making her look like a dissatisfied child. Make-up completed, she slammed the door behind her and hurried along the street to join a straggling bus queue at the corner.

It was a day like any other in what she considered a boring existence. The days dragged with monotony, little to distinguish one from the other. Like today, she thought. The bus will be full and I'll have to strap hang all the way to the office.

As she had predicted, when the bus turned the corner, the passengers filled the aisle, shoulder to shoulder, and grudgingly shuffled along to allow the others to board. Her fist closed around an empty strap and she glanced at one of the more fortunate passengers who had managed to get a seat. He pored over his newspaper, held in front of him like a shield, awkwardly turning the pages in the limited space.

Looking over the man's shoulder, Carol skimmed the headlines, impatiently waiting for him to select another page. When he did, it was full of advertisements and special offers. The bus, too, was festooned with garish pictures of products and the hoardings flashing by on the roadside were plastered with commodities, urging everyone to buy . . . buy . . . buy.

Advertising is a curse of the times we live in, she decided. Just like that letter this morning, she thought, specially designed to catch the reader's attention.

Some firms use gimmicks like that, sending personalised letters telling the recipient to ring this or that telephone number, promising something to their advantage if they complied with the request. It really was an invasion of privacy, she reasoned, stepping off the bus and hurrying to the office, her mind now filled with the more practical things of the day.

After a hectic morning, Carol and her friend, Julie, spent the lunch hour in the park as they did every day, enjoying a brief respite away from the office while sharing their sandwiches with the insistent ducks that crowded around their feet quacking loudly to attract attention.

'Just look at this,' Carol said indignantly, pointing to the brown paper wrapping on her lunch. 'Advertising glaring at you everywhere you look. No one can escape from hard selling, not even at home.'

'Had a salesman round knocking at your door, did you?'

Julie glanced sideways at Carol as she crumbled crusts and scattered them on the ground.

'No, just some con letter in the post this morning along with all the other junk mail.'

'What did it say?'

'Oh, just to ring a number to hear something to my advantage.'

'Are you going to?'

'Not likely. There'll be pushy salesmen at the other end trying to sell vacuum cleaners or saunas or something I definitely don't want.'

'I couldn't leave it like that,' Julie

4

said, 'I'd have to ring, just to make sure. You never know — it could be a bone fide letter.'

'Fat chance!'

Carol threw the offending brown paper wrapper into the litter bin, casting aside any possibility that the letter may be important by the decisiveness of her action.

However, the first thing she noticed that evening when she sank into her armchair and kicked off her shoes, was the crumpled ball of the letter lying on the carpet. Remembering what Julie had said, she leaned forward and grabbed it, smoothing the paper on her knee. Perhaps Julie was right, maybe she should ring to find out. Feeling a little foolish, she dialled the number. A crisp voice answered almost immediately, to her surprise as it was past office hours.

'Welwyn, Carter and Dodson. May I help you?'

'I had a letter from you this morning asking me to get in touch. My name is

Carol Trevallan.'

'Ah, yes, Miss Trevallan, we were hoping you'd ring. Mr Dodson is dealing with the Morrissey estate. One moment please and I'll put you through.'

Light classical music filtered through the ear-piece, serving little to calm Carol's curiosity. The Morrissey estate, she thought. What's that? And what on earth has it got to do with me?

'Dodson here.'

The mellow tones halted her speculation.

'Good of you to call, Miss Trevallan. Is there any chance that you could come to our part of the world so that we could meet face to face and discuss our business? I'd rather not go into details on the telephone. We'll reimburse any expenses, naturally.'

Carol glanced at the address on the letter heading — Cornwall, miles away!

'Well, I'm not sure that . . . '

'Combine business with a little

pleasure,' the voice soothed. 'My secretary will book you into a charming little hotel here in Falmouth and we can arrange to meet at my office. Can you travel on Saturday, stay for a week or so, at our expense, naturally? There are plenty of diversions here to keep you happy during your stay.'

This was sounding better by the moment Carol thought mentally totting up if she had enough money in her bank account for the fare.

'It sounds intriguing,' she said. 'But can't you give me some idea of what this is all about?'

'All will be explained when we meet, Miss Trevallan. It really is much too confidential and complicated to discuss on the telephone. Look, I'll get my secretary to confirm your hotel reservation by post, then I'll contact you first thing Monday morning and arrange an appointment. Leave you to settle in over the week-end, eh?'

What sounded like a friendly chuckle accompanied the words, rattling into

Carol's ear and leaving her even more frustrated.

'Farewell and look forward to meeting you very soon,' Mr Dodson said in a hasty farewell, then replaced the receiver, leaving Carol gaping into the mouthpiece.

She sank back in the chair trying to remember everything he'd said and realised with a start he'd said nothing of the nature of the business that was to take her across country to Cornwall. But whatever it was, there was a free week ... maybe two ... of holiday involved. She'd be a fool to pass this up.

Later, spooning beans over toast, she reviewed her wardrobe and the spiralling cost of renewing it, eventually deciding on buying what she deemed were a few new necessities. Carol's excitement grew by the minute. Not only the mysterious holiday, but new clothes. What more could a girl want?

Another letter waited on the mat when Carol groped her way from the bedroom a couple of mornings later.

Rubbing her eyes, she seized it, instantly awake when she read the postmark. Another letter from Cornwall! A banker's draft for two hundred pounds had her instantly awake, her eyes glued to the letter.

' . . . for your immediate expenses . . .' she read aloud.

The print jumped off the paper. She read the name of the hotel, Traveller's Ease, and her imagination soared. Skipping around the flat, she hastily dressed and left to start what promised to be an exciting day.

Finding herself ahead in the bus queue was an omen and when for the first time she managed to get a seat on the crowded bus, she instantly decided that life had definitely changed, for the better. She couldn't quite believe her luck was changing, hopefully for the better.

The lunch hour was designated for cashing the bankers' draft and shopping. Between forays into the various stores, she gulped down a sandwich.

Ten minutes later, she returned to the office, breathless and lumbered with a collection of carrier bags. She requested leave of absence for the next two weeks, but only her friend Julie had been let into the secret of her mysterious expedition to Cornwall.

'Do be careful,' Julie urged. 'They still have white slavers, even in these modern times. You don't know anything about this mysterious Mr Dodson. He could be the front man in a white slave ring!'

'You've been watching too much television,' Carol replied and grinned at her friend.

They shared a conspiratorial giggle but Carol remembered the words later in the week as she packed her case ready to leave. The excitement of the trip waned as she wondered what this was all about. And why was it happening to her?

The whole business was a puzzle. She had racked her brains to try to recall if the name of the estate mentioned by the Cornish lawyer should mean anything to her, but nothing had come to mind.

What if she had a long-lost relative who had passed away, leaving her some vast fortune!

Oh, stop being silly, she admonished herself, and concentrated on finishing her packing.

* * *

The countryside grew greener by the minute as the train sped out of the city. Years ago, she had made this journey with her mother and father who both loved the west country.

They'd gone there every year for holidays while she was growing up but in her early teens, life had changed. The holidays came to an end as did her happy childhood when both parents were killed instantaneously in a tragic car crash.

The ensuing years had numbed the pain but staring out of the window at the unfolding beauty of the journey had evoked the poignancy of that terrible time when she believed her life to be empty and meaningless without her mother and father.

It would have been different had there been brothers and sisters. She would never have felt so alone as she had in the intervening years but the distant aunt who had taken her in had been the only relative who came forward at the time to offer Carol a home.

Carol remembered her Aunt Maisie with great affection. Much older than her parents, she had done her best to provide for her, giving all the comfort and love she'd needed to help her over the terrible tragedy. Life had dealt Carol another blow when her aunt died leaving her on the threshold of her first job after leaving school.

Everyone had been so kind at the time, promising to keep an eye on her, urging her to take any problems she encountered to them with assurances that she need never feel alone. But it hadn't been like that as the weeks passed by.

Once the funeral was over, everyone slipped back into their well-ordered lives and Carol had to face the prospect of moving from her aunt's rented house when the owner put it up for sale. She'd found the tiny flat after a hectic search and from then on, her life had been caught up in the dreadful rut of monotony.

There had been casual dates during the last six years but no young man had held her interest for long. Girl friends had found their mates and settled down, thus Carol had become a loner.

She gazed out of the window, weighing up her life. She was not unhappy. It just seemed that she was unfulfilled, in a job that required the minimum of brains and with few, if any, real friends. She'd tried the usual things, joining clubs, sporting activities but none of these had appealed, neither had they filled the void. I suppose life is boring because I'm boring was her assessment. She shrugged. So what!

Someone sat down heavily next to her and bumped her arm.

'Sorry . . . the motion of the train,' the newcomer said as he excused his heavy landing.

Carol turned to meet the gaze of large brown eyes that reminded her of liquid velvet, under a shock of dark brown hair, neatly slicked back from his forehead. She smiled, dismissing the collision and turned back to the window.

'It's so smoky down there,' he said, nodding to the back of the train where he'd been earlier. 'When they didn't come round with the oxygen masks I thought it was time to leave.'

She looked at him again, returning the smile. She fancied there had been the hint of an accent, and he volunteered the information.

'Over from the States, on holiday. I'm making the most of the time to try and trace my ancestors. We're into that in a big way back home. Guess that's because we have so little history of our own, we want to latch on to what our forebears left behind when they emigrated. Logical,' he convinced himself and Carol with a nod.

'Did they come from Cornwall, your ancestors?' she asked, sensing he was waiting for some comment.

'Seems so. I have a letter of introduction to a firm down there who've got some information for me. Sounds good, too. I can hardly wait to see what they've discovered.'

Carol smiled and turned to the window once more feeling the topic was exhausted but the friendly young man was speaking again.

'You on vacation? I understand lots of folks regard this place as a great area for recreation.'

Carol sighed. She'd rather be left alone with her thoughts, painful though they were, but it seemed the American was reluctant to let the conversation lapse.

'Maybe two weeks,' she said shortly. 'Hope the weather keeps nice.'

How boring she sounded. Embarrassed, she smiled again, mustering a little more friendliness.

'I hope you're enjoying your holiday over here. The weather helps,' she added lamely.

'Sure am,' he said with spirit. 'I've done the usual things — Tower of London, trip up the Thames, art galleries, museums. Guess I sound like a pretty square guy, eh?'

Carol laughed out loud. Pretty? Handsome, she'd call him. His brown eyes had sparkled as he related his list.

'Not at all,' she protested. 'Those are the kind of places I like to visit, too. You'll find plenty to interest you in Cornwall. There's a great deal of history there. Did you know they used to mine tin? I think that's all at an end now but the trade goes 'way back into the middle ages. There are museums with all the details.'

'Right! I'll look into that. And what about you?'

He veered the conversation her way again.

'Staying with friends? I noticed you're alone.'

'No. Just a break from monotony.'

Carol wondered what else she could say. The trip was shrouded in mystery and she'd have to wait until Monday to find out the real reason for her visit.

'Perhaps we'll meet up. I'm staying in Falmouth. I understand it's not too big a town.'

Carol started in surprise, tinged with a shiver of delight.

'Me, too. I'm staying there, too,' she added. 'It's possible we'll meet. Not many main streets to cover.'

She grinned, the prospect looking rosier by the minute.

2

The Traveller's Ease stood in one of the main thoroughfares of Falmouth, a narrow, winding street full of shops, right in the heart of the bustling town. Only the illuminated sign outside bore evidence that an hotel nestled there.

Inside was a small foyer resplendent with gilded fittings and wall lights that were reflected in the mirror-festooned walls, giving the ground floor a more spacious air. A wide staircase led to the main body of the hotel which sprawled over the heads of several of the adjacent shops.

Carol was fascinated at the show of opulent splendour, so discreetly hidden from outside. At a first glance she decided it was a far better hotel than she could ever afford. More likely she would have opted for a humble boarding house. Her heart skipped a beat. Suppose something untoward happened and she was left with the bill for the holiday? It would take her months to pay it off! She was immediately put at ease by the clerk at the reception desk.

'Miss Trevallan? Ah, yes. You're Mr Dodson's guest. Room Fourteen,' he said with a beaming smile of welcome.

His fist walloped a bell and a liveried porter appeared from nowhere to carry her cases upstairs while the receptionist indicated the lift. By the time she arrived at her bedroom door, the porter was already carrying the cases inside.

Carol crossed to the window and peered into the bustling street below. It was thronged with holidaymakers, ambling along the narrow paths and impeding the flow of others when they paused to gaze at colourful displays in the shop windows.

Through a gap in the buildings opposite, she saw the silver glint of the sea caught in the rays of the sun and the swirling flight of complaining gulls.

Hugging herself with pleasure, she turned to look around the room but as she did so, a movement in the street below made her look through the window again.

A hooting taxi was struggling through crowds. It stopped at the Traveller's Ease, the door opened and the tall handsome American from the train stepped out, smiling as he glanced around, obviously delighted, as she had been, at what he saw.

Carols' eyes widened. What would happen next! It seemed the talkative American was to stay at the Traveller's Ease, too! This could turn out to be a most interesting holiday, she thought.

★ ★ ★

She met up with the American later, in the dining room. It was buzzing with conversation from the many holiday-makers. The tall, young man hovered at the door until he was shown to his table.

Then, looking around the room, he caught sight of Carol and said something to the waiter who made a bee-line through the tables to where Carol sat studying the menu.

'The American gentleman asks is it possible for him to be seated with you? I can make some excuse if madam prefers to sit alone,' he said quietly, leaving the suggestion hanging as he waited for her response.

Carol smiled across the room to the American who sat waiting. It would be pleasant to have company, she thought. Catching his eye, she nodded and he rose instantly, skilfully weaving his way through the tables until he was beside her. Even the waiter seemed pleased.

He beamed from one to the other and edging away to a discreet distance, waited their summons.

'I'm Carol Trevallan.' She shook hands and remarked, 'I didn't think we'd meet again so soon. Quite a coincidence, isn't it?'

'Mark Hambel.' He grinned. 'A happy one I'd say. Looks like we're destined to spend some time together, the way fate keeps intervening.'

Carol smiled. Lucky me, she thought, looking forward to the next two weeks with unmitigated pleasure.

After dinner, they strolled down to the jetty where the outgoing pleasure boats boarded and sat on a bench watching the moonlight dancing on the blackened sea. Conversation had been mostly one-sided during dinner and Carol deduced that Mark Hambel was from a rich, influential family back home in Boston.

He spoke of holidays at the Cape, his horses and told her of exploits in his red coupé, dwelling long on a trip he'd made across country to the Grand Canyon.

She had been content to listen goggle-eyed and impressed by what sounded to be a glorious life style, so unlike her own, so when Mark asked what she did with herself, Carol merely shrugged and skilfully evaded the question.

'Let's do some window shopping,' she suggested.

Ambling through the streets, where many shops were still open for the holiday trade, they came upon a curious window display in a tiny side alley. Worn and battered looking articles — brooches, medals, bronze jugs, a tiny spindly-legged table, all jostled for space with fishing rods, gaily-coloured plastic balls, children's buckets and spades.

'How odd,' Carol remarked. 'It's as if the proprietor couldn't make his mind up whether to sell antiques or holiday goods. What an interesting shop. I'd love to look inside.'

She peered through the window and fumbled on the door catch but it was securely fastened for the night.

'I'll come back another time,' she said wistfully, turning to Mark but he was already moving on along the street.

She glanced at the faded gilt lettering

above the window, THE TREASURE CHEST.

The name ignited her imagination and she was loath to move away but when she did, her mind was made up. She'd come back another day and hopefully the shop would be open, then she could satisfy her curiosity and browse to her heart's content. Mark stood waiting a few steps away.

'Come on! We'll come back on Monday,' he said.

Carol thrilled at the familiar we. It sounded as if he intended to spend more than a little time with her but when he embarked on yet another tale of his exploits, her interest waned and she began to think that Mark Hambel was a young man obsessed with the sound of his own voice, and it had begun to grate on her nerves.

* * *

On Sunday, the town was even more crowded with day trippers adding to the throng milling along the narrow walkways and loitering in front of the shop windows. After an early breakfast, Carol joined the procession in the street below, eager to explore and, more importantly, find where the offices of Welwyn, Carter and Dodson were situated where she was to attend at Mr Dodson's summons to be informed of the reason for her visit.

Her footsteps took her along the same route as she had walked the previous evening and when she came across The Treasure Chest in the alley, she was delighted to see that a light burned inside.

Shielding her eyes with the palm of her hand, she pressed her face close to the glass and peered through into the dingy gloom. There was a blur of activity at the rear of the shop and the shape of a man could be seen moving to and fro.

Biting her lip in anticipation, her fingers trembled on the door catch as she eased it from its cradle. The door swung open and gingerly, she stepped inside. A bell tinkled, startling her as she closed the door and at the same time, from the far end of the shop, a man's voice cried, 'Sorry, miss, but we're not really open.'

Carol hovered a few feet inside the shop, squinting in the near darkness to locate the owner of the voice. The man stepped from behind a tiny counter at the rear and walked swiftly towards her, snapping on all the lights as he passed them.

He wasn't much older than Carol, perhaps in his late twenties and only a few inches taller. Tousled hair, streaked by the sun, fell in unmanageable locks over his forehead, above blue eyes that were the hue of a clear summer sky.

'Sorry,' he said again with a rueful smile that deepened the cleft in his chin.

'No, it's all right. My mistake.'

Embarrassed at her intrusion, she turned to leave.

'It was just, when I saw the light

inside, I thought . . . I passed this way yesterday and it seemed such an interesting shop. I was dying to look inside, and so disappointed it was closed so when I saw the light this morning . . . '

She shrugged, her words trailing as she looked at him with a rueful smile.

'Nothing to stop you having a look, I suppose,' he said hesitantly.

He looked around himself as if seeing the shop for the first time.

'It is fascinating, isn't it?'

'Such a mixture of goods.'

The young man nodded, his expression suddenly sombre.

'Uncle Jim could never make up his mind whether to collect antiques or go along with the holiday trade, so he tried to have the best of both worlds, hence the jumble.'

'The shop belongs to your uncle?' Carol asked, her eyes widening.

'It did. He wasn't my uncle really. I just called him that. He was more like a father, grandfather even, to me. He died a while back.'

'Oh! Sorry,' Carol mumbled. 'I suppose you're keeping an eye on the place then,' she ventured and when he nodded, she went on, 'Are you going to open up again soon? I can see you're in the middle of cleaning.'

Her eyes strayed to the broom he had rested against the counter when she came in.

'Afraid not. The shop is nothing to do with me really. He wasn't a relation you see, just a friend. I don't know who owns The Treasure Chest now but I still have the keys Uncle Jim gave me and I come in from time to time, usually on a Sunday morning, like now, just to keep the place from rotting away under the dust.'

Carol was weighing what he had said.

'Surely the shop must belong to someone. You'd think they would step in and take over.'

'Uncle Jim didn't leave a will and he doesn't seem to have any descendants. Never married you see, no children. He was the last in his line of family as far as we know.'

'How strange,' Carol muttered staring at the young man whose face suddenly tightened. 'I'm Carol Trevallan by the way.'

'Seth Coombes.'

His smile altered the contours of his face. Earlier sad and downcast, it was now radiant.

'Come on, if you're really interested in the old place let me give you a guided tour.'

He waved her to follow and Carol did, to the rear of the shop into a tiny stock room.

'Just look at this.'

He pointed to a shelf where boxes were piled almost to the ceiling, each stencilled **Children Buckets and Spades**.

'I reckon Uncle Jim must have got them cheap. Always had an eye for a bargain. Trouble was, he had no head for selling things once he bought them. Like these for instance.'

He pointed to a stack of boxes marked **Postcards**.

'They'll never sell up here.'

Carol looked at the boxes. Though they were old and battered, they seemed sturdy, belonging to an age when even packaging was made to last.

'There's loads more stock stacked away upstairs that hasn't seen the light of day for years. It'll be quite a headache to sort through it all.'

She followed Seth into the body of the shop.

'I'd better lock the door. Don't want anyone coming in.'

He hurried to the door and she made to follow, halting in her tracks when he said over his shoulder, 'People might think we're open if they see the lights on.'

She was suddenly embarrassed again, feeling the colour rush to her cheeks.

'Like me,' she said quietly. 'I'm sorry. I'd better go and let you get on with your cleaning. I'm interrupting your work.'

He raised a hand to forestall her.

'No, I didn't mean that. It's just . . . well, I'm not supposed to be here myself. Officially the shop is closed for the duration. The solicitors have all the keys until they sort out who the shop belongs to. They didn't know Uncle Jim had given me one. I just kept it for a souvenir really, then one day when I came to check the place was OK, I came in for . . . '

He shrugged, sighing as he hung his head.

'For old time's sake?' Carol suggested.

Seth nodded. 'Uncle Jim was good to me. I miss him very much.'

'I know. Me, too.'

When he looked at her with surprise, she told him about her Aunt Maisie.

'I still miss her, too.'

Ambling around the shop, Seth pointed out the various coloured balls suspended from the ceiling.

'Fishermen's weights. These are lobster pots. I've never been sure whether

31

they were for sale or decoration. They're a throwback to Uncle Jim's father who owned the shop before him. Spent most of his time at sea. They do add atmosphere to the place though,' he said thoughtfully, casting his eyes over the collection. 'Anyway, what are you doing here in Falmouth? On holiday?'

Carol smiled.

'Sort of. I have to see a solicitor tomorrow on business.'

The statement sounded like a closed door to their friendly exchanges of a few minutes earlier. Realising that, she was about to tell him of the strange letter and even stranger telephone call when Seth turned to look at her squarely.

'Do you fancy a cup of coffee? There's a nice little café nearby. We can sit and talk. Make the most of the good weather.'

Carol nodded. The idea of spending some time with Seth appealed to her, even although they had just met.

'But let me help you tidy up first.'

Seth shook his head.

'All done. I'll just put these out of sight.'

He grabbed the broom and a duster and disappeared into the back room, reappearing after a moment, shrugging his arms into a jacket. Switching off the lights on his way to the door, Carol noticed how his eyes seemed to melt as with an inscrutable expression, he glanced around the shop before they left.

The tiny café was busy but they managed to find a recently vacated table in a corner. Sitting across the table from one another Carol asked, 'So what do you do when you're not sweeping out your uncle's shop?'

'Fishing mostly. I help out on a trawler, the Sabrina. There's not much else to do here unless you're caught up with the tourist trade.'

'Sounds as if you don't approve of us.' She smiled.

Seth shook his head.

'It's not that. I'd just like to have

made a go of the shop. It could be a little gold mine but Uncle Jim was too old and tired to be bothered any more and well . . . '

He shrugged.

'You've seen the place. It needs a lot of money spending on it to compete with the other shops around here. I'd have liked to specialise in the antique trade. I used to go with him to auctions at Truro and farther afield. Picked up a bit of knowledge on the way and from the books I got out of the library. But like I said, Uncle Jim just seemed to want to live out his days in peace. 'I've had my time son,' he used to say to me. 'Your day will come, then you can do what you like with the old place.''

Carol sat up, leaning across the table.

'That sounds as if your uncle really intended you to have the shop.'

Seth grinned ruefully.

'I know, but he never left a will you see, so there's nothing I can do about it. So what business exactly is it that brings you to Falmouth?'

She told him of the letter, laughing about throwing it away when she'd thought it to be merely another sales gimmick.

'But it was when Mr Dodson invited me to stay for a week or two whilst we discuss business, I thought it was too good a chance to miss so, here I am.'

Her triumphant wave seemed to encompass the town as she smiled gleefully.

'Did you say, Mr Dodson?' he asked.

She nodded, wondering why his mouth had hardened into a straight line and his eyes, once blue and sparkling, now glittered like cold steel as he glared across the table.

'So that's why you came snooping round the shop, is it? You came to see how much money you could make out of it when old Dodson hands over Uncle's keys.'

He pushed back his chair and stood up abruptly, looking down at her.

'Nice to meet you, miss, whoever you are.'

With that, he stomped out of the café, slamming the door so violently that the waitresses halted in their service and stared after him.

3

Carol wandered back to the Traveller's Ease in a daze wondering what she had said to make Seth's attitude change so abruptly. It had to be something to do with mentioning Mr Dodson. Was he the solicitor who held the keys for the shop? Perhaps the Morrissey estate was the solicitor's way of referring to the shop.

Despite the morning sunshine, now warm and embracing, she shivered at the thought. Tomorrow seemed so far away and she must wait until then to find out what this was all about.

She was relieved there was no sign of Mark when she entered the hotel foyer as the last thing she wanted right now was his constant chatter about his possessions and exploits. Taking the lift upstairs to her bedroom, she waited until lunchtime, hoping he'd gone off for the day on one of his expeditions.

She was glad to find the table set for one when she entered the dining room. The waiter quickly came to her side and filled her plate.

'The young American gentleman was sorry to miss you at breakfast. He's gone off on a boat trip up the estuary.'

Carol nodded, smiling with satisfaction as she began to pick at her meal, though her mind was troubled as she mulled over the events of the day so far.

It was too nice to stay indoors, so on leaving the dining room later she made her way outside to explore the streets once more, determined to steer away from The Treasure Chest lest there would be another confrontation with Seth Coombes.

It was with some surprise that she stumbled upon the offices of Welwyn, Carter and Dodson in one of the streets leading out of the town. There, on a window, emblazoned in large gold letters, the firm of solicitors advertised their presence.

Earnestly wishing it was tomorrow, Carol stared for a moment at the auspicious offices before retracing her footsteps to the hotel.

Mark Hambel appeared at dinner, slightly flushed after his day in the sun. Under his arm he carried a weighty guide book which he placed with great ceremony on the table beside his plate. Tapping it with a finger tip he beamed at Carol.

'Great little book — lots of interesting snippets of information about Cornwall. Did you know the Navy press gangs used to hide in these narrow streets to force men aboard their ships as crew?'

He paused for full effect staring wide-eyed at Carol across the table.

'And the packet ships sailed from here to America with rich cargoes. They were often raided by bloodthirsty pirates on the way. Fascinating stories. I wonder if my ancestors travelled by packet boat.'

'Have you discovered any more about them?'

Carol sat forward, her interest aroused fractionally.

He shook his head and said shortly, 'Tomorrow.'

★ ★ ★

The waiter was clearing away Mark's breakfast dishes when Carol came into the dining room the next morning. She was glad she didn't have to face him as the prospect of meeting Mr Dodson had kept her awake most of the night and she dreaded another lecture, interesting though it was, on the fate of erstwhile sailors.

It was as she was preparing to return to her room that the waiter summoned her to the telephone.

'A gentleman wishes to speak to you,' he said, handing her the receiver.

'Good morning, Miss Trevallan. Mr Dodson here. Hope you've settled in all right. Nice little place, I'm sure you'd agree. I do hope they're looking after you.'

Without giving her a chance to comment, he went on.

'About our little get together. Sorry I can't make it until tomorrow. Something rather urgent has come up. Anyway, it will give you another day to enjoy the local scenery, eh?'

The cackling laughter grated on her ears in much the same way as the information had yet further unsettled her nerves. Another day, she groaned, another day to wonder why on earth I'm here.

With the appointment set for ten-thirty the following morning, Mr Dodson excused himself once more then rang off leaving Carol totally deflated, and no nearer to discovering the reason for her summons to Cornwall.

Leaving the hotel, she wandered down to the quay to watch the fishing boats come in, loaded with their catches of pilchards. The salty tang of the sea

41

blended with a powerful smell of fish as the crews hoisted heavy baskets dripping with brine and trailing fronds of seaweed on to the quayside.

Stepping over ropes and pools of sea water, she ambled along the jetty looking at the catches, gleaming like silver in the creels. Carol was enthralled. She could almost taste the sea on her lips caressed by the fresh wind coming off the water.

'Alongside, Seth.'

A voice boomed from the hold of one of the trawlers and she turned to watch the young man she'd met the day before, skilfully coiling ropes and throwing them on to the quay as his boat glided into the harbour. He jumped ashore and made fast the ropes assisted by another of the crew. It was as he straightened up that he saw her and a deep flush coloured his already weatherbeaten face.

Carol smiled somewhat nervously, unsure of whether or not he would acknowledge her presence. She was relieved when at last, he gave the curtest of nods before carrying on with his work.

She watched, fascinated at the dexterity of the crew which had the load ashore in minutes before hosing down the deck, slimy from fish scales that glittered like sequins. One by one the fishermen gathered their belongings, hailing one another in noisy farewells as they climbed the slopes to the town.

Meanwhile, on the quay, traders, armed with clipboards and stubs of pencils, bartered with the skippers until they had mutually agreed a price with a symbolic handshake. Carol was so captivated by the scene that she failed to see Seth standing at her side until he spoke.

'Er . . . sorry about yesterday,' he said gruffly, looking down at his rubber boots, as if too embarrassed to meet her eyes. 'It's not your fault,' he went on. 'If you are one of Uncle Jim's lost family then . . . '

Carol's hand reached out to touch his arm, recoiling when she felt his sodden sweater. He grinned.

'Imagine I don't smell too sweet either.'

'Look,' she began, 'I don't know why Mr Dodson wants to see me. His letter came out of the blue, and it's a complete mystery. As far as I know, I don't have any links with Cornwall except that Mum, Dad and I used to come here year after year for holidays when I was young. I couldn't possibly have anything to do with your uncle or his shop, and I wasn't snooping,' she added more firmly. 'I was genuinely interested. I thought the shop was like an Aladdin's cave. I still do.'

Seth was still looking down, his thumbs locked in the pockets of his soiled jeans.

'Do you think we could start again?'

As he raised his head, a slow smile eased away the lines around his mouth.

'I'd like to buy you another coffee to make amends and this time I'll stay long enough to pay the bill.'

Carol grinned, her shoulders relaxing when she realised the animosity between them from their previous encounter had evaporated.

'Sounds like a good idea to me.'

She turned, expecting him to follow but he hesitated.

'Not like this. I'll have to go home and change. Fancy a walk through the town? I'll show you where I live and you can wait. Won't take me long to clean up.'

As they walked, Carol told him about her work, grumbling about the dreadful monotony and explaining why she had been thrilled to have the offer of a fortnight's holiday.

'My parents and I used to come here every year but I don't ever remember seeing The Treasure Chest.'

'It's been here through several generations of Uncle Jim's family, so he used to tell me. There was only him and his brother and neither of them married but their father came from a big family.

That would be back in the mid-1800s. Lots of people left the area then, looking for work. Packages to the States were cheap and we lost a lot of good Cornishmen seeking their fortunes abroad.

'Uncle Jim said his father had mentioned some of the family had left home. Broke his grandmother's heart, he said, as they never heard from them again, whether they were settled or even dead. Sending letters wasn't as easy in those days and no doubt some people couldn't read or write so it's understandable that families lost touch with one another when they went off to distant lands like America.'

'I met an American on the train,' Carol said, remembering. 'He was telling me his roots were in Cornwall. He was hoping to trace his ancestors. Wouldn't it be strange if he turned out to be one of your uncle's long-lost relations?'

They both considered the possibility silently as they climbed the hill but eventually Seth shook his head.

'Doubt it. That would be too much of a coincidence,' he said shortly, but the seed had been sown in Carol's mind and she wondered.

So many unusual things had happened to her recently. Nothing would surprise her, even the coincidence that Mark Hambel could be a descendant of Seth's Uncle Jim's long-lost family.

A row of tiny cottages stood on the crest of a hill with a magnificent view of the harbour estuary. Here the air seemed to have the zing of champagne about it, Carol thought, breathing deeply and glorying in the sweep of the sea. There was a medley of colours, from the deep blue of the sea, greying where the sand banks loomed in the water, to the varying shades of green and purple of the distant countryside.

Seth opened the gate of one of the windswept gardens, frowning at the tumble of wildflowers and grasses that grew in profusion, some almost as high as the fence.

'I haven't much time for this,' he said frowning. 'Neighbours tell me my father used to be a keen gardener. Grew the best roses in the row. But I've never had a feel for it myself.'

His eyes raked the horizon and Carol could see where his heart lay when she, too, looked at the rest of the fleet of trawlers sailing homewards.

By now, they were inside the cottage and Seth indicated a chair, excusing himself as he left her alone. The room was clean and sparkling, showing the abundance of care that the garden lacked. Gleaming brasses on leather straps hung from either side of the fireplace and the mantel was covered with a collection of framed photographs, some old, in shades of sepia.

In pride of place was a family group of a smiling man and woman with a child on her knee and she wondered if this was Seth's parents. She was holding the picture when he came downstairs, his hair dark and wet and the fresh smell of soap wafting around him.

'That's my parents. Shortly after that, Dad was lost when the Homebird went down and Mum . . . well, she was never the same again. Followed him soon afterwards, of a broken heart, some said. Uncle Jim took me in. He was on the Homebird but he was one of the lucky ones the lifeboat picked up. Said he felt he had a responsibility to look after me. Don't know why. We weren't even related. Said he felt guilty that he should be spared whereas so many family men were lost.'

Carol replaced the picture with the others, her heart heavy as she pictured the smiling little boy on the photograph, suddenly without either his father or mother to care for him.

'You must have been devastated when they both died. Do you remember much about it?'

He shrugged.

'I suppose I was too young to realise. Hardly remember my parents at all, only Uncle Jim.'

His face brightened as he pointed to a photograph of a white-haired old man with an irrepressible twinkle in his eye that even the photograph had not diminished.

'He used to take me out on the boat with him on school holidays but all that came to an end when his rheumatics got the better of him. Devoted all his time to the shop then. His brother had passed away and we moved into the rooms up above. I loved it there but the stairs got the better of him and when he got the chance to buy this cottage he snapped it up. It's only a couple of doors away from the one where I was born. Mind you, Uncle Jim used to complain like blazes about the long climb up the hill every day!'

'So this belongs to your uncle, too?'

Seth shook his head.

'Luckily he made it over to me a few years back. If he hadn't I'd have been well and truly on the streets. Old Dodson says I'll be lucky to keep it if the new owner disputes the transfer.' He shrugged. 'I'll wait and see. Not much I can do about it now.'

Carol recognised his dilemma. The scenario was similar to what her own had been when Aunt Maisie died, and she had found herself homeless. She glanced at Seth, pulling on his jacket as they prepared to leave, and earnestly hoped that life wouldn't deal him any more heartaches than he'd already suffered.

4

The offices of Welwyn, Carter and Dodson resounded with various activities. Telephones rang intermittently and the rhythmic patter of fingertips on keyboards gave an aura of a busy office.

Carol, needing all the confidence she could muster, had dressed carefully for the meeting with Mr Dodson. She had chosen to wear one of her new outfits, a navy linen suit with a crisp lemon blouse but despite feeling smart and businesslike, she still felt overawed when she walked into the office. The receptionist appeared to have been expecting her.

'Mr Dodson's waiting for you, Miss Trevallan. That door, over there,' she said pleasantly.

Carol tapped then went in. The portly man stood up and offered his hand, his smooth, rounded face creased in a welcoming smile.

'How nice to meet you at last, Miss Trevallan.'

He pointed to a chair and Carol sat down, perching nervously on the edge. She was aware that his sharp eyes had missed no detail as he scrutinised her carefully. She glanced around the well-appointed office.

One wall was stacked to the ceiling with all kinds of books. Sunlight infiltrated the room despite the vertical blinds that were open at an angle and the huge desk, behind which Mr Dodson sat, was slatted with sunshine and shadows.

After a few polite enquiries as to how she was enjoying her stay at the Traveller's Ease, Mr Dodson, all trace of friendliness cast aside, in a business-like manner, launched into the topic of his summons.

'I've asked you to come here to discuss the Morrissey estate and its implications regarding your good self,' he began, opening a manila folder in front of him and examining the sheaf of papers inside. 'Our researchers have made extensive enquiries to trace the descendants of William Henry Morrissey who died in 1873.

'His large family spread all over the globe, some as far afield as South Africa but as a result of the various global conflicts, epidemics and so on, many of his forebears were either killed or died of natural causes leaving only the offspring of Henry Clive Morrissey and Edward Sefton Morrissey, his brother. These are the only ones we've been able to trace with any accuracy.'

Dodson sank back in his leather chair and peered at Carol over the top of his spectacles, drumming his fingertips together in a silent tattoo.

'Henry Clive left a daughter, Isobel, whom I believe was your great-grandmother,' he went on, then he paused and looked closely at Carol who was speechless with amazement, scarcely believing what he said.

'There must be some mistake,' she

said. 'Are you saying I'm the only one left?'

'Not exactly. There is another contender, as it were.'

He grinned.

'There's the American side of the family. You may have met him at the Traveller's, a Mr Hambel. A personable young man with a lot to say for himself.'

He laughed, rather self-consciously Carol thought, as he glanced again at the papers on his desk.

'He appears to be the great-grandson of Edward Sefton's daughter. As he was the eldest surviving son, the Morrissey estate may well fall to him alone but as there is a lapse of so many years between the demise of William Henry Morrissey and now, the executors of the will have deemed it advisable that we consult both surviving parties to discuss the estate while they try to reach some informed decision.'

'Does this concern the shop, The Treasure Chest?' Carol asked quietly.

Dodson nodded slowly, waiting for her to go on.

'I came across it quite by chance and I've met Seth Coombes. There doesn't seem to be much worth fighting over. It looks very rundown. What about Seth . . . Mr Coombes? He said his uncle, Mr . . . '

'Mr Morrissey, the only surviving grandson of William Henry,' the solicitor prompted.

'What Mr Morrissey said to Mr Coombes made him believe that he was leaving him the shop.'

'Ah! If it were only that simple,' Dodson said slowly, his voice pronouncing each word like the toll of a death knell. 'Alas, in the absence of a will left by James Morrissey, there are procedures which must be followed stringently. The shop could well have been inherited by him had there been no known survivors. He could have no doubt proved the word of mouth intention of William Henry, the man who raised him. However, enquiries have revealed that there are two possible heirs, yourself and Mr Hambel, so this countercedes any claim Mr Coombes may make on the estate.'

Carol found the solicitor's slow smile impossible to decipher. She sensed his feeling of regret that she and Mark had appeared on the scene and wondered if he would have been more satisfied had Seth Coombes inherited The Treasure Chest. It was a sentiment she could understand, having nurtured similar feelings herself.

'Incidentally, the shop is not the only bequest,' Mr Dodson went on. 'There is far more at stake than a dilapidated store.'

By now Carol was completely at a loss for words as she listened intently to every word he said. The information had both dismayed and excited her but that she could be involved was too much to register in a brain that was unable to focus properly.

'What happens now?' Her voice was trembling. 'And what about Mr

Coombes. Is his claim dismissed? It seems so unfair that he is deprived of what his uncle ... Morrissey ... intended to be his.'

'Alas! Too many people die intestate. It creates so many complications. If only everyone looked ahead and put their affairs in order, outcomes that some parties may consider to be unjust, like this for instance, could be well and truly avoided.'

'You said there was more involved than The Treasure Chest.'

'Ah, yes, but I'm not at liberty to discuss the whole issue at the moment. I'll arrange a meeting with you and Mr Hambel in a few days, then we can go into the matter in detail. Until then, my dear young lady, enjoy your holiday. There is so much here to interest holidaymakers.'

Mr Dodson's voice droned on but Carol wasn't listening. Her mind was teeming with a torrent of possibilities and suppositions. He had stood up and was ushering her to the door before she realised it. Shaking hands, he promised to contact her soon.

Her legs were shaking, matching the tremors of her heart, as she went outside but throughout her own discomfort, she thought of Seth Coombes and the part he played in all this.

Yesterday, she and Seth had strolled through the streets and bought a lunch of cheese rolls and soft drinks which they'd eaten sitting on a grassy mound overlooking the sea. Although she and Seth had chattered like old friends until then, now they were both silent, as if in a private world with nature as the seagulls swirled above them, dipping and diving over the waves.

'What will you do if you suddenly find yourself to be the owner of a Cornish shop?' Seth asked quietly.

Carol frowned, turning to look at him but his face was in profile as he gazed out to sea and she couldn't hazard a guess at his reason for asking the question.

'I really don't know,' she said

honestly, her mind tumbling with possibilities. 'I suppose I could give up my job and move here but I don't know anything about running a shop. Anyway, as you pointed out, it needs a lot of money spending on it and I only have what I earn each month. So, I expect I'd have to put it up for sale and . . . oh, I don't know!'

She looked at him again, dismayed to see that the lines around his mouth had hardened and his eyes narrowed as he stared distantly to the horizon. An invisible wall had sprung up to divide them.

'That would be the end of The Treasure Chest,' he said, 'the end of an era. Oh, I daresay it would be snapped up, not for the sake of the shop. All the stock would be scrapped. But its location, in the heart of the town, makes it valuable property. There are lots of developers ready to turn these old places into holiday homes, cafés, offices, anything to make money. Poor Uncle Jim. I wonder if he's looking down on us. He really loved that old place.'

'If he is aware of what's going on, then I bet he wishes he had left a will,' Carol said quietly, unable to meet Seth's eyes, she felt so guilty at the possibility that she was robbing him of what was intended for him.

★ ★ ★

She had agreed to meet him again, after her visit to Mr Dodson. She numbly suffered the constant chatter of Mark Hambel over lunch, distracted as she looked forward to meeting Seth again to tell him about her visit to Dodson's office.

Mark, too, had kept an appointment with the solicitor but it seemed to be the fact that he had successfully traced another branch of his family tree that fired his enthusiasm, rather than the possibility that he was to inherit a share in the Morrissey estate.

'It'll only be worth peanuts,' he said

scornfully. 'Best thing to do is put it on the market for a quick sale and whatever else there is, can you see it being worth anything? I say turn whatever it is into cash and get on with our lives. I'll hand my share of the business over to the lawyers, and let them take charge of the transaction. Then they can send me a cheque after they've taken their cut. Knowing what lawyers are like, there won't be much left.'

Though she had never met him, a vision of Seth's benevolent Uncle Jim flashed into Carol's mind and she cringed, wondering what he would be thinking if, as Seth had imagined, he was looking down on it all.

'What do you think? Sensible thing to do?' Mark was saying.

Carol shrugged. The whole affair was beginning to get to her.

'Let's wait and see,' she said cryptically, pushing back the chair from the table as she prepared to leave, unable to bear his brashness a minute longer.

To her dismay, he did the same and followed her from the dining room and downstairs, tagging along uninvited.

'I'm going to do a little shopping. I want to buy a present for my friend,' Carol said, hoping to excuse herself but Mark merely grinned.

'Fine! I'll walk along a little way with you. We haven't seen too much of each other the last couple of days. I was rather hoping we could have got together.'

His wide smile held a wealth of meaning and Carol marvelled at the change in her feelings. When she'd first met him, she had been overwhelmed by his interest in her but now, she couldn't wait to shake him off.

It was not to be so easily achieved as when the time for meeting Seth approached, the gregarious Mark Hambel still dogged her footsteps.

Nearing the King's Pipe, where Carol and Seth had arranged to meet, Mark pulled a guide book from his pocket.

'Say, there's a great story here about this old monument. Did you know that the King's Pipe was used by the revenue men for destroying all the illegally imported cigars and tobacco 'way back? Looks just like a chimney! Interesting, eh? I guess even in the olden days those guys recognised what a money maker they had with their taxes on smokes. The King's Pipe, eh? Now I wonder which king that would be.'

He consulted his guidebook, thumbing rapidly through the pages, leaving Carol to slip away unnoticed, so absorbed was he in the information he gleaned.

Seth was waiting, leaning idly on the wall of a nearby shop.

'Come on,' she said, urgently taking his arm and pulling him out of sight. 'I've been trying to get away from my transatlantic friend for ages. He's driving me potty with his collection of guidebooks.'

Seth laughed, allowing himself to be

led off hastily, round a corner.

'So, how did your meeting with old Dodson go?' he asked, slightly out of breath with their speedy retreat.

He took Carol's hand and the action was momentarily disarming, leaving her hesitant and tongue-tied.

'I . . . I may be one of the heirs, and so might he, the American.'

Seth stopped in his tracks and faced her.

'So you were right.'

He sighed.

'Well, I suppose I'd better congratulate you, though, like I said before, the shop's only worth the ground it stands on.'

He tugged her on and Carol wondered, should she mention that Mr Dodson had said there was more at stake than an old store? For the time being, she decided she'd let it rest there.

The day was glorious, there was so much to do, and best of all, Seth was squeezing her fingers tightly. A thrill ran through her body. People were far more important than possessions and as far as she was concerned, Seth was the first person she'd ever met who had made her feel almost special.

5

Mark Hambel greeted Carol at dinner as soon as she entered the dining room.

'What happened to you this afternoon? When I looked for you, you'd suddenly disappeared into thin air.'

'I thought you would follow me,' Carol said truthfully, omitting the fact that she'd taken steps to make sure he did not.

'I went on over to take a look at Pendennis Castle,' he said. 'Did you know it was built by Henry the Eighth when he was fighting the French and fortified by Queen Elizabeth the First in case of invasion by the Spanish? Gee! Imagine, still standing today, some achievement.'

He ate ravenously and for this Carol was grateful, for it meant she was spared any more of his tourist blurb. Blessed with a good appetite herself, tonight the meal held little interest, as she was still wracked with guilt about stealing Seth's inheritance. She looked slyly at Mark who was now tucking into his dessert and wondered how he would react to what she was about to say.

'I've been thinking about a young man I met called Seth Coombes,' she began. 'James Morrissey brought him up when both his parents died. Seth said that Mr Morrissey had intended the shop, The Treasure Chest, to go to him but unfortunately he didn't leave a will.'

She paused noting that Mark was watching her intently, frowning as she spoke.

'I think it's most unfair that we step in, out of the blue, and take The Treasure Chest away from him. After all, neither you or I didn't even know his uncle, well, the man he called his uncle, Mr Morrissey.'

She breathed a sigh of relief now that she'd said it. Mark wiped his mouth with the napkin with a look of distaste, glaring as he stared hard at her across the table.

'What can we do? It's in the hands of the lawyers. I guess he could make a claim but if he was no relation . . . '

He shrugged.

'Anyway, you've seen the old place. We both have. It's a run-down dump. Split three ways they'd have to pay us in postage stamps once it was sold.'

Carol wondered if Mr Dodson had told him there was another side to the inheritance, much more valuable than the shop, if she had interpreted his words correctly. She ignored the thought and went on.

'I still think we should do something for Seth Coombes. He was hoping to open up the shop and explore the antiques side of it.'

'How come you know so much about this guy?'

'I met him when I went back to the shop. He told me all about it.'

'And he claimed the place belongs to him?'

'No, it wasn't like that. He was very fond of Mr Morrissey and he simply told me that the old man had . . . '

'Tell him to see the lawyers,' Mark said abruptly.

'Mr Dodson said the estate could well have passed to him had no descendants turned up.'

'So this guy has a grudge against us for stepping between him and the loot. Guys step out of the woodwork when there's money up for grabs. It's my bet there'll be others like him trying to stake a claim. Situations like this prompt people to hover like vultures.'

His voice was charged with bitterness.

'The chance of getting their hands on some easy dough brings out the worst in people,' he said and stood up, dismissing the conversation.

His curt refusal to pursue the subject left Carol feeling quite angry and frustrated.

'I'm staying for coffee,' she said with an edge to her voice and was relieved when he excused himself and marched out of the dining room without a backward glance.

Carol lingered over her coffee trying to analyse her feelings for Seth. She admitted to herself that she had grown fond of him and, judging by the way he now frequently took her hand, wanting to spend more and more time with her, she suspected he was not indifferent to her. But where was it going, she wondered.

In another week, perhaps less, the business of the estate would be settled and she would be going back to her life in the city. She might never see Seth again. The thought filled her with dismay. She considered the possibilities that would be available to her should she inherit enough money to stay on in Falmouth permanently. Would Seth want her to do that, knowing she had, however innocently, taken away what so rightly belonged to him?

With a troubled heart, she wandered down to the quay where they had arranged to meet at a bar. Outside tables, covered with gingham cloths, afforded a splash of colour on the dingy courtyard and strings of coloured lights, strung from the lamposts, were like necklaces of glass beads, completely transforming the busy quayside into an almost magical place. He hailed her from one of the tables, standing up to greet her as she drew near.

'I ordered you a lemonade,' he said reaching for the unopened bottle on the table and removing the top. 'I've got some good news. Well, not so good as it means I'll miss a trip out with the trawler and my wages will be docked but I'll be ashore all day tomorrow. We can go somewhere for the day.'

The prospect lightened Carol's spirits as she gazed into his eyes, shining in the reflected light from the multitude of lights. Her heart skipped a beat whenever they met and she realised that the fondness she had admitted earlier had blossomed into love. She'd gladly follow him anywhere he suggested. She smiled, trying to keep her feelings in check.

'That's great,' she said. 'Where shall we go?'

Over the rim of his glass he grinned.

'That's my surprise. Wait until tomorrow.'

They strolled arm in arm through the gaily-lit streets, window shopping and enjoying the holiday atmosphere. Shyly, he put his arm around her waist as they turned into a quiet lane and Carol looked up at him, waiting for the kiss she knew would come. Every word they had said, each moment they had spent together, had been leading to this and she was as eager as he, when their lips met.

Drawing apart, they gazed into one another's eyes, each surprised at the subdued passion they had experienced, then Seth drew her to him again, kissing her with more spirit than before. Carol found herself being carried along on the tide of emotion that coursed through her body, weakening her knees until they felt like jelly as she clung to him.

Her fingers strayed through the mass of hair that curled at the nape of his neck and she breathed in the spicy masculine smell of him that intoxicated her senses.

She never wanted to let go. This was where she wanted to be, in Seth's arms for ever.

'My love,' he whispered, 'don't go.'

Her eyes widened as he went on, snuggling his mouth in the softness of her hair. She felt the heat of his breath on her neck.

'Don't leave Falmouth. Stay with me. I can't bear the thought of losing you now that you've come into my life.'

Carol was sobered by the words. What would her life be if she came into a vast amount of money, even the shop? Maybe that would stand between them instead of bringing them more closely together. The events of the next few days would make decisions easier. At least then she would know what was involved.

Would Seth still want her? A more terrible thought racked her heart. Did Seth only want her now because she might inherit the shop? Was that the reason for declaring his love? After all, she reasoned in cold clarity, we've only known each other for a couple of days.

She pulled herself free of his arms and smiled.

'I think it's time for me to go in. Perhaps we can talk some more tomorrow, if you still want to,' she added, suddenly shy.

He leaned forward and kissed her cheek.

'Yes,' he whispered, squeezing her so tightly she could barely breathe. 'I want to. I'll see you on the quay,' he called as he walked away leaving Carol troubled with the disquieting thoughts her mind churned up to fray her newly-found happiness.

There was another surprise waiting when she went into her bedroom. A note from Mark Hambel had been pushed under her door.

Late message from Mr Dodson. He wants to see both of us tomorrow morning at nine. I'll see you at breakfast and we can go on there together. Mark.

6

Seated across the desk, Mr Dodson was a formidable figure. His bald head glistened in the sunshine filtering in through the vertical blinds and now and then glinting on his gold wristwatch and signet ring.

Peering over the top of his steel-framed glasses, lips pursed together, he regarded them thoughtfully before he spoke and when he did, the rich tones of his voice held Carol captivated as, breathlessly, she wondered what information he was about to impart. Sitting uneasily on the edge of a high-backed chair, she clasped her fingers together so tightly that the nails dug into her palms.

Impatient and anxious, she chewed on her bottom lip, longing for this pompous man to get on with the business in hand instead of treating them as if they were on trial scrutinising them and no doubt summarising their eligibility as potential heirs to the Morrissey estate. Shuffling on her chair seemed to spur Dodson on and he smiled across the room, nodding to each in turn.

'Well, Miss Trevallan, Mr Hambel, I have now completed one part of our investigation regarding the content of the legacy.'

He paused and stared from one to the other, prolonging their anxiety.

'There is a considerable fortune at stake here.'

Flicking through papers on his desk without even glancing at them, he went on.

'When Mr William Henry Morrissey died in 1873 he had, unknown to his immediate family, invested a large amount of capital in the tin mines at Tregwyn. These have, of course, been closed for a number of years now but the dividends he accrued from his investment were banked by the family group of solicitors who were managing his finances at that time. The original income, with the accumulated interest over so many years, has now reached a startling figure.'

He leaned back in the chair and tapped his fingertips together in the mannerism that Carol had found irritating when she first met him. Taking off his spectacles, he paused long enough to polish them with a white pocket handkerchief.

The waiting was unbearable. Breathlessly she waited for him to go on but to her surprise it was Mark Hambel who spoke next.

'And who is the rightful heir?' he asked in a matter-of-fact tone. 'Have you found out yet? Seems to me that's the most important thing right now.'

Mark leaned forward on the edge of his seat, listening with rapt attention to every word the solicitor was saying. His lips were tightly pressed together and his hands curled into a ball on his lap, the knuckles white with tension. He glanced briefly at Carol, but she looked away. The whole situation was so far removed from her normal life, that she felt it was all happening to someone else.

Me, an heiress to pots of money! Not a chance. There's got to be a snag somewhere, she thought.

By the time they left Dodson's office, still neither she nor Mark had been told the exact amount of the money involved. When Mark had introduced the subject of who was the rightful heir, the solicitor had clammed up, stating that as soon as their investigation of that aspect of the law was completed, he would be in touch.

In the meantime, he said that he would treat them both as having an equal share. Outside, Mark frowned as they walked through the streets into the town.

'Seeing that we've got this far, I don't think that either one of us should hog all of the dough. No matter who comes out on top, we could agree now to sharing the loot. What do you say? Shall we make a bargain?'

He stared at Carol, waiting for her assent to his proposal.

'After all, that lawyer guy said there was a considerable fortune. There should be enough for both of us.'

She shrugged, still not believing her part in any of it.

'Whatever you say,' she said shortly, anxious to be away now to meet Seth.

'So that's it then?' Mark persisted. 'We agree to share the dough no matter what happens?'

Carol nodded but before he could speak again, she hurried off, calling over her shoulder, 'I have to go now. I'm meeting someone. I'll see you later.'

Seth was sitting on the harbour wall and came forward to greet her, his tanned face softening under a smile as he swept back the hair from his forehead.

'So, how did it go? Successful meeting?' he asked, seeming genuinely interested.

Carol sat down beside him, feeling a blush prickling the neck of her blouse when she remembered their kisses of last night. Shivers trickled like icy rivulets down her spine when Seth took her hand, waiting for her to speak.

'We're still no wiser. It seems that they're still looking into the matter. I'm tired of all this speculation,' she said. 'I just wish it was all over and I can get back to leading a normal life.'

'And will your life include me?' Seth asked quietly, squeezing her fingers.

She knew he was looking at her but didn't turn to face him as she said, 'Everything's happened so quickly. I don't know what the future holds for me. Seems like I never did. Losing my parents . . . Aunt Maisie . . . getting turned out of the house and fending for myself . . . most people my age have family around them, to advise them.'

She stopped, embarrassed at her outburst, remembering Seth was alone, too. He had no one. She looked at him.

'I'm sorry. Things like this don't

usually happen to people like me. Everything is so mixed up right now. I can't even think straight.'

Seth's response was to wrap his arms around her in a fierce hug that almost dispelled the air from her lungs. Kissing her brow, his lips were like the gentle brush of a butterfly's wings. He stood up, pulling Carol to her feet.

'Let's put all this to one side and get off and enjoy ourselves. We've got to make the most of what's left of the day.'

By his feet was a sturdy haversack. He picked it up and shook it. There was a chink of cans and the rustle of paper.

'Our picnic. See how domesticated I am? You'd be getting a good husband.'

Carol's mouth gaped.

'Is that your idea of a proposal, Seth Coombes?' she said flippantly. 'Not exactly traditional is it?'

'It just slipped out.'

He grinned.

'Actually I was saving it for later. However, I can do it in the old time tested way if you like.'

He bent to one knee and clasped the haversack to his chest. Passersby were grinning as they walked along the jetty, turning round with wide smiles of encouragement and jocular remarks. Carol's face was scarlet with embarrassment. Yanking him to his feet by the straps of the haversack, she frowned.

'Everyone's looking at us. If you don't stop this minute I'm walking off and leaving you.'

Chuckling, Seth slung the haversack over his shoulder and took her hand again as they began to trudge up the incline into town.

'I'd follow you,' he said with a gleam of mischief in his eye. 'You're much too valuable a prize for me to allow you to escape.'

Carol followed, still smiling at his antics, but the words lingered. Maybe, if she was an heiress, it would be worth his while to hold on to her. Was that what he meant? The words hurt, twisting in her heart like the blade of a long, sharp knife.

7

The morning sunshine had brought the holidaymakers out early from their hotels and boarding houses and the streets were thronged with people making last-minute purchases before they headed for the beaches. There were queues at all the cafés. Seth grinned as they filtered through one of the queues straying on to the narrow footpath.

'See how well prepared I am? We've escaped all this.'

He shook the haversack thrown carelessly over his shoulder.

'I hope there's no queue at the bus stop.'

Carol had a sudden memory of the morning bus queue she encountered on her way to work every day and she smiled, gripping Seth's hand. Even standing beside him at the bus stop would be a pleasure. There was no one waiting by the roadside halt sign and Seth groaned.

'Oh, no! It looks like we've missed the bus. And there's not another one going this way for an hour.'

He put his arm around her shoulder and looked into Carol's eyes.

'What shall we do? Go somewhere else or kill time for an hour?'

She smiled, conscious only of the pressure of his arm.

'The destination was a secret if you remember so what can I say?'

She laughed as his eyes sparkled obviously remembering his words of the previous evening. Before they could decide what to do, a voice hailed them from the other side of the street.

'Hi there, Carol!'

Mark Hambel strutted across the road walking swiftly towards them with a triumphant smile playing around his mouth as he waved the ever-present guidebook. A premonition of doom darkened Carol's heart as the joyful day she had envisaged alone with Seth suddenly crumbled with the likelihood of Mark Hambel tagging along with them uninvited, complete with his wretched guide book. With considerable effort, she tried to hide her frustration.

'Oh, hello, Mark. Are you off somewhere interesting?'

'Yeah! Well, I sure hope so. I've just hired an automobile to explore the countryside in these parts. I hear there's an interesting ruin of a tin mine ways out a little. Seems like a good place to go. Catch up on some local history.'

He looked quizzically at Seth and paused.

Carol realised she was remiss in not having introduced Seth and as she did so, she wondered anxiously if Mark would make some comment about the Morrissey estate and Seth's involvement.

Nervously she waited for his reaction, remembering his earlier annoyance

when Seth's name had been mentioned.
However, the American lumbered forward amiably with an arm outstretched,
his eyes shielded by heavy sunglasses.

'So!' he said shaking hands, 'this is
the guy you were telling me about. Glad
to make your acquaintance.'

He grinned.

'Seeing as you're a local, maybe you
can advise me where to go. This guide
book's not too good on road maps.
Maybe I'll have to buy me a route
directory from somewhere.'

His eyes strayed over towards the
various shops before coming to rest on
Carol's tense face.

'Better still, why don't you come
along? There's plenty room in the car
and we could have a great day out
together.'

He linked his arm through Carol's,
ignoring Seth's frown.

'What do you say?'

As they settled in the car, Carol in
front and Seth, openly scowling, in the
back seat, Carol tried to remember

which of them had agreed to come along with Mark but she was at a loss to recall that either of them had said anything. They had been skilfully coerced by Mark.

Seth gave directions from the back seat and soon they were out of Falmouth and travelling along leafy lanes that twisted and turned. Carol looked into the driver's mirror and caught sight of Seth.

He grinned and shrugged, obviously determined to make the best of things.

'Left at the next junction,' he prompted and Mark slowed down to negotiate the turn. 'It's not far now. There's a museum and an old shaft you can explore, with a pricey admittance charge. But I know of another mine, not completely developed, that you can wander in and out of. I think there's more to see there, and it's free.'

He grinned into the rear mirror, catching Carol's eyes.

'Not many people know about it as it was never completely developed so we could have it to ourselves.'

Mark swivelled in the driver's seat.

'How about it, folks? The museum or the mine?'

Carol eyed the guidebook tucked away in the dashboard compartment and inwardly cringed, imagining Mark reading lengthy passages aloud as they walked around the museum.

'The old tin mine sounds interesting,' she ventured, 'and we can look for a place nearby to have our picnic. I hope there's enough for three.'

She grinned, turning to look at Seth and waiting for his approval. He nodded.

'OK! It's about another two miles or so down this road and sharp left. I'll warn you about the turn off when we get nearer,' Seth said with a smile.

For a while they drove in silence, Mark and Seth concentrating on the road ahead and Carol lost in her thoughts as she gazed out of the window. The countryside was beautifully lush and green. Wild flowers cheered the hedgerows with their presence and leafy trees overhung the lane for sections making a lacy network to dapple their faces as they passed.

Carol remembered an outing from years ago when her parents had taken her as a child, to run unleashed among the bracken, of the Cornish moors before dishevelled, hot and sticky, she had settled down beside them to munch her way through mounds of sandwiches and chocolate biscuits that melted in her hot, grubby hands.

The memory evoked tears that stung her eyes and she blinked them away as she gazed through the window again at the countryside, fleeting past her like memories.

The car slowed at Seth's command and Mark turned left. Only a few yards down the lane they came across the old mine shaft, half hidden among trailing weeds. When Mark finally brought the car to a halt, Carol scrambled out and flexed her shoulders, upturning her face to the warmth of the sun.

'How quiet it is,' she said. 'It's as if we've discovered another world, undisturbed for generations. No traffic . . . nobody around . . . '

'Mother Nature at her best,' Seth broke in, smiling at her display of contentment.

'I can imagine it's not always been like this,' Mark said, looking around reflectively. 'I guess there's been a few hearts broken here, and pocket books. The guys who were mining and had to call it a day for whatever reason,' he explained, 'they probably lost the shirts off of their backs. No doubt there's a few tales these crumbling old walls could tell.'

He began to thumb through his guidebook, humming softly as he pored over the pages. Carol raised her eyebrows, catching Seth's eye and he turned away grinning. Gazing at the entrance to the old mine shaft, his face wrinkled with a frown.

'It's years since I've been here. I remember getting a rollicking from

Uncle Jim the last time I came. There were three of us. We'd biked here with a bottle of water and some sandwiches. One of us, I can't remember who it was, had a ball and we started kicking it around, the way kids do. Then suddenly my mate disappeared. We heard a rumble, like distant thunder, and then a cloud that looked like smoke came out — over there.'

He pointed to a mound a little way off.

'We were scared witless, didn't know what to do. But before we could really panic, he appeared from the shaft covered in white dust, for all the world looking like a ghost. Seems the ball had fallen into a pothole and he'd climbed in after it.'

'He wasn't hurt?' Carol asked.

'Only bruised and shaken up. Scared, too, like we were. We jumped on our bikes and pedalled home as if the devil was after us. When I told Uncle Jim what had happened he was furious. That's the only time I remember him being angry. He took my bike away and locked it up for a whole month. Said we could have had a tragedy on our hands.

'Seems like there's lots of these potholes around. Apparently they were meant as ventilation shafts. Maybe they weren't successful. That could be why the mine closed. Making a fortune out of mining tin's no use if you're buried alive,' he said thoughtfully, his eyes scanning the environs of the mine. 'I'm beginning to think this was a bad idea to come here. It doesn't feel right.'

'Maybe we should have settled for a visit to the museum,' Carol suggested glancing at Mark but he was so engrossed in his guidebook, totally oblivious of the conversation.

'Well, we should be all right just so long as we watch where we're going and not take any stupid chances.'

Seth glanced around with an air of uneasiness betrayed by the line on his brow. By now Mark had tucked the guidebook in his pocket and slotted the sunglasses into the pocket of his shirt.

'Lead on,' he said to Seth. 'Show us the sights.'

Seth shrugged and began to point out where the runways, carrying the mined ore, had stood. Old trestles were stacked in a rotting heap with ancient battered buckets and some abandoned tools. He began to pick up a spade.

'I wonder who this belonged to,' he said thoughtfully weighing it in his hand.

'Some guy long dead and buried,' Mark suggested. 'Maybe his folks or their descendants still live in these parts.

He glanced around as if expecting to see some visible proof. Meantime Carol was chilled by the images drifting through her mind, spurred on by a vivid imagination.

'I think it's rather spooky here to be honest. I wish we hadn't come now. I can picture all those men, long ago, hard at work and frustrated when the mine had to close.'

She shivered despite the sunshine.

'Just imagine them going home . . . '

'Sweat trickling down their faces,' Seth interrupted laughing.

'Well, yes, it would be like that,' Carol said seriously. 'Probably they had wives and children waiting at home for money to buy food and shoes. It must have been very hard in those days trying to earn a living. It reminds me of a churchyard, this place, and tombstones covered with flowers. Maybe it's a fitting memorial to the men who worked here, whoever they were.'

Treading carefully, they ventured a little farther afield where mounds of soil, brought up from the mine decades earlier, stood like giant molehills, now covered with grass and wild flowers through the passing years.

To a casual passerby they seemed merely a part of an undulating landscape but Seth pointed them out for what they were. Nervously, he glanced around.

'With all this soil and rock, hewn out of the mine, there must be huge cavities inside. I wonder how good the miners were at propping up the roofs. It could be that the ground beneath our feet is pretty hollow. Uncle Jim was right,' he said decisively chewing on his bottom lip. 'This place is dangerous. I should never have suggested coming here.'

'Yeah! Maybe but seeing as how we're here now, we may as well give the place the once over,' Mark said walking to the mine entrance. 'Let's have a look see inside.'

He snapped his fingers, turned and ran back to the car, calling over his shoulder, 'I saw a flashlight in the compartment.'

He returned after a few moments, waving a torch.

'I'll go in first to light the way. You guys follow me.'

Carol hesitated but spurred on by Mark, she, too, ventured inside. Seth loitered at the entrance.

'I don't think we should do this. Don't go in. It's much too dangerous,' he said warily.

Carol was inclined to agree but hesitantly waved to Seth, urging him to follow.

'We'll only go in a little way.'

Tentatively groping the damp walls, she followed Mark who was a dark shape a few yards ahead, the ray of his torch like a long stick flitting from side to side as he carefully picked his way along the narrow tunnel. Where the beam of light struck the rocks, stones glistened like silver and gold, gleaming with prisms of a myriad of colours.

Carol turned to see how far behind Seth was but to her dismay, she saw his body silhouetted against the entrance as he drew fingers through his hair in an attitude of indecision.

'Seth!' she called. 'Come on. It's really quite safe. It's quite beautiful down here. The colours are really gorgeous. Why don't you come and see for yourself?'

There was a roar from somewhere behind her and she blinked as dust powdered her head. Somewhere in the distance she heard Seth's urgent cry but the words were lost in vibrations as, ominously, the roof began to crumble around them.

Mark had turned and was scrambling back down the tunnel towards her, stumbling over loose stones and piles of earth heaped against the sides of the narrow channel.

'The whole lot's coming down,' he yelled. 'Let's get out of here.'

Grabbing her shoulder he twisted her round to return the few yards they had come but it was too late. Only a few feet in front of them, the entrance was blocked by a huge pile of rocks and loose earth that cut out the daylight!

The rumbling, like passing thunder, died away slowly, leaving the air dense with cloying dust that made breathing grate on the lungs. Carol felt a rush of panic trickle down her back in icy cascades and it seemed her heart had risen to her throat when she became aware of the overpowering blackness that had suddenly engulfed them. A cold sweat covered her brow and her mouth seemed full of grit.

'Mark,' she said, croaking through parched lips. 'Where are you? Are you all right?'

She tensed her arms and legs, testing for sprains. Reassured that she was not injured, she almost gagged on the dust, coughing violently to clear her throat. But what had happened to Mark? Her voice rasped his name as she choked on the dust.

'Mark! Mark!'

There was a sudden movement not far away from where she stood, cowering against the side of the tunnel and she began to grope forward, hands and fingers splayed before her as if sleepwalking. In an instant the powdery dust became a white fog as Mark switched on the torch.

'I dropped it,' he spluttered. 'I've been rooting around on the floor looking for it. Are you OK?'

'Yes . . . yes. What about you?'

'OK. Where are you?'

Suddenly their fingers touched in the gloom and Mark grabbed her hand. His own was trembling.

'Let's sit down for a minute and try to get our bearings.'

His breath was as shallow as her own as they both gasped for air.

'Maybe Seth can use one of those old shovels he found to dig us out.'

He glanced at the mountain of earth between them and the route they had come along the tunnel.

'Maybe it's not as deep as it looks,' he said hopefully.

Silently they looked at the soil and rocks that effectively formed a barrier between them and safety outside. It was a formidable obstacle and neither voiced their doubts, desperately trying to assure themselves that help would come eventually.

'I'll turn off the flashlight for a moment, just in case the batteries run out. There's no knowing how long it will take him to move all that.'

He glared at the fallen roof. Then

they were thrown into pitch blackness again when the light went out and Carol felt Mark's arm slip round her shoulder. She realised he was as scared as she and wondered briefly if the comfort of their closeness was for his benefit or hers.

'Do . . . do you think there's enough air in here?' she asked hesitantly, feeling the choking panic rising like tight bands across her chest, restricting her breathing into hollow gasps.

'Sure there is. Didn't Seth say something about there being ventilation shafts. We'll be OK. Anyway, they'll get us out of here before long.'

Carol noted the tremor in his voice and, not reassured by the words, wondered what he was truly thinking.

'What time is it?' she asked, her voice echoing in the darkness.

The beam of light from the torch strayed momentarily on to Mark's watch then was gone again.

'Just after one o'clock.'

'They'll be serving lunch at the

Traveller's Ease,' Carol murmured pensively. 'I wonder if they will miss us.'

She was surprised by the pangs of hunger gnawing in the pit of her stomach, or was it fear?

'Will anybody at all miss us?' Mark said quietly. 'After all, no one knows we came here, only Seth.'

There was an ominous silence before he went on.

'It would suit his purpose to let us rot here. If he did that, both the heirs to the Morrissey estate would be out of the way in one fell swoop. Then he could step in and claim the lot. You heard what that old guy, the lawyer said. There's a chance it would have all gone to him anyway if they hadn't traced us.'

Carol leaned forward, cradling both knees with her hands. The thought of Mark's arm around her shoulder made her cringe and she was glad to feel the release when his arm slipped away.

'Seth wouldn't do that,' she said, a tone of indignation rising in her voice.

'Anyway, someone would see the car. It's out there, in plain sight of anybody travelling along the road. That would have to be explained.'

The very idea was too preposterous to dwell on . . . or was it? Disbelief niggled the far regions of her mind.

'The car would be easy to dispose of. He just drives it out of this area and dumps it somewhere else. When they eventually discovered it, the police would start off looking in a totally different place. By the time they got here, if they ever did, we'd be long gone.'

'You're talking nonsense. Nobody would do that. Seth's not like that at all,' Carol argued.

'How do you know, honey? Seems to me you're as much of a stranger round these parts, as I am. Remember, you've only known this guy a few days. You can't know much about him, only the bits of information he's fed you. How do you know what he's really like?'

His voice rose in anger causing

undeniable tendrils of fear to claw at Carol's heart. Her only answer was to snort at the wild accusations but Mark had not finished yet.

'When there's money involved, believe me, honey, no matter how nice a guy is, his personality changes. Have you ever stopped to wonder why he's attached himself to you? He knows you're in line for a share of the loot. That's why. Could be his interest's simply mercenary.'

He paused before saying quietly, 'Not that you're a beautiful, young woman, but, well, you know what I'm saying here. You catch my drift.'

His fingers squeezed her arm and Carol drew away involuntarily, cringing at his touch. She knew what he was saying all right. Hadn't the same thought crossed her mind? But Seth's not like that, she told herself over and over again, trying to appease her doubts.

'If he's trying to get us out then we should hear some sound of the spade moving on the rocks,' Mark said in a cynical tone.

Carol held her breath, realising he was doing the same but the only sound was the ominous trickle of falling soil from somewhere nearby, grating on her nerves like the constant drip of a tap. She felt the movement of Mark's body beside her and after a moment he nudged her arm.

'Here, take this. I've found some gum in my pocket.'

She wanted nothing from him, not even conversation and was about to tell him so with a sudden flash of anger, when he added, 'It'll stop your mouth being so dry.'

His fingers found her hand and she felt the gum pressed into her palm and briefly wondered about the picnic Seth had carried in the haversack. He'd left it in the car. It was the stimulation she needed.

'The car keys,' she said with a triumphant air. 'Seth couldn't drive the car without your keys.'

A low chuckle greeted her words.

'Honey, the doors are unlocked and starting a car without keys is no trouble. You just spark the wires together. Easiest thing in the world.'

His voice droned on as Carol continued to listen for some sound of Seth coming to their aid. But no sound could be heard — only Mark's voice droning on.

★ ★ ★

Carol's head ached. A constant throbbing hammer seemed to strike right through to the brain, pounding relentlessly behind her eyes in a mixture of colour. Raising her head was difficult and she winced, as an arrow of excruciating pain shot down her spine.

'Oh, my head,' she moaned softly rubbing both temples with her finger tips.

'You've been asleep,' someone said.

With a start, she remembered. It was Mark who had spoken and with cold clarity, she realised where they were. Nothing had changed. They were still prisoners in the disused tin mine. He switched on the torch and in its glow his face seemed demonic, hollow shadows on both cheeks and a wild glare in his red-rimmed eyes.

'Your boyfriend has deserted us,' he said defiantly. 'Just like I said he would.'

She ignored the statement, bottling her freshly roused anger.

'What time is it?' she asked.

'A quarter after three.'

She gasped.

'How could I sleep with all this going on?'

She eyed the mountain of rocks in front of them.

'Shock maybe. Think I dozed off myself. Anyway, now we're both rested we should try to do something to help ourselves.'

'Like what?'

'As I see it, we have two chances. We could continue along the tunnel and maybe find us an air vent or we could tackle this.'

He nodded to the barrier of rocks.

'It'll be hard work and there's a risk we may set the fall off again, but it may be our only chance. What do you think?'

8

Carol looked behind, along the tunnel in the direction they had been walking. Mark shone the light but its beam did little to raise their hopes. The gloom ahead seemed endless as the tunnel bored its way through the earth, disappearing in the distance in a dark blur.

'I don't fancy going any deeper inside,' she murmured. 'Even if we find a shaft, we have no way of getting out. I'd prefer this way.'

She indicated the mound of fallen roof.

'Yeah! I'm with you.'

He rose to his feet, tottering a few steps on unsteady legs as he went closer to examine the obstacle. He called over his shoulder.

'If we move the rocks at the top maybe we can squeeze through.'

'And what if it starts falling again?'

Carol knew there was no answer as she, too, rose falteringly to her feet. Mark switched off the torch and they both swayed towards each other until they joined hands in the darkness.

'The trouble is, we'll be digging blind. The torch is sure to give out on us before long. Damn that guy, Seth.'

The tone of his voice altered.

'He should have had help here before now, even if he'd walked out of here.'

Carol was inclined to agree and her heart sank at the possibility of Seth's betrayal. Mark was right. Seth had only shown an interest in her when he knew she was a claimant to the Morrissey estate. He must feel very strongly, even fanatically about his own dubious claim if he was prepared to kill for it.

She shivered uncontrollably, trying to still her chattering teeth as a premonition of their eventual doom rose to haunt her. She felt Mark press the torch into her hand and heard the soil scattering at the crunch of his feet as he began to clamber up the mound of rubble.

'I'll let you know when I'm at the top then you can shine the flashlight to give me some idea of where it's best to make a start.'

'Be careful,' she urged, clutching the torch tightly in a clenched fist.

The menacing sound of falling rock seemed to fill the tunnel and Carol fumbled for the switch. Mark, too, had heard it and he paused, halfway up the landfall.

'Listen!'

Carol signalled him to remain still, perched unsteadily as he was on the fallen boulders.

'I can hear something. The roof's coming down again.'

A scream froze in her throat and the only sound now was their heavy breathing as they prepared for the worst. A metallic tapping that seemed miles away had their spirits rising in seconds when they recognised a rhythmic tattoo from the other side of the barrier.

'There's someone there. Listen, Carol! Listen!'

Holding their breath, they heard the welcome sound.

'We should make a signal, too,' Mark said breathlessly. 'Let them know we're still alive.'

Carol flashed the torch around but all that she could see were rocks.

'There's the torch,' she said dubiously, 'but nothing else.'

She was scrabbling among the rubble, not sure what she was looking for. Mark half slid down the pile to stand beside her.

'Yes, there is.'

He fumbled in a pocket and withdrew the car keys.

'We'll try this.'

The tapping had stopped and he seized the opportunity of the silence to beat out a morse code signal of S O S. Scarcely daring to breathe, they waited for some response and it was not long in coming. The tattoo quickened. Their signal had been heard!

'Maybe we should stand back away from the fall . . . sit down and wait,' Mark said.

He pulled Carol a few yards farther down the tunnel and they sat, backs against the moist walls, waiting with hope lightening their thoughts.

The dull whine of machinery reverberated through the tunnel and when it stopped, intermittently, Carol fancied she could hear the welcome buzz of voices. She rested her head against the dank walls and closed her eyes, sighing. It couldn't be voices, she reasoned. Not yet . . . but soon . . . maybe . . .

She shivered, knowing that she might have been trapped here for ever, her breath ceasing when the air was used up. Who was there who would have mourned her passing, she asked herself? No one. Her parents gone, Aunt Maisie, too, there would only have been her friend, Julie, from the office and she would never get to know what had happened because her body would never have been found.

She could have been entombed here, until the end of time. She shivered again.

Realising she was being carried away by her vivid imagination, she mentally gave herself a shake to dispel the disquietening thoughts. However, thinking of Julie sent her mind off on another tack. When she disappeared without trace, Julie would tell all their colleagues at the office that Carol had been snatched by white slavers. She could almost see now, dabbing at her eyes as she related the tale, a break in her voice when she stopped to weep.

I did warn Carol. Take care what you're doing, I said. This man you're going to meet could be the boss of a white slave ring. You could wake up in some foreign land . . . in a harem or something. But did she listen to me? Oh, no. And now she's gone, vanished without trace. I did warn her before she went off on this wild goose chase and now I'll never see her again.

Carol found herself smiling and felt slightly foolish, grateful, for the first time, that the darkness hid the silly grin on her face. Perhaps this is what happens, she thought. If you're locked away somewhere in a situation like this, you just steadily go mad. She must remember to tell Julie about her wild imaginings. But there were voices now. This time she had not mistaken the buzz.

She held her breath, listening. Mark nudged her and she knew he, too, had heard them. He switched on the torch but its light was dull and faintly yellow, doing little to light up their gloomy surroundings but affording them some company and consolation.

A trickle of soil began in a cascade, racing down the heap of the landslide. Stones were falling, bouncing along the ground with momentum, some missing them by inches. Mark stood up and dragged Carol slowly to her feet.

'Let's get on farther down the tunnel. We're likely to get hit by the rocks when they push through.'

There was a joyous lift to his voice and Carol's spirits, too, rose as she realised, hopefully, they would soon be out of this miserable place. They sat down again, a few yards deeper inside the tunnel. Mark sprayed the now flickering beam of the torch on the rocky barrier.

'They can't be far away now.'

He grabbed Carol's hand in a vice-like grip and her fingers closed round his fist as the joy of relief flooded her spirits. A sudden dazzling flash of light shone on their faces and they turned their eyes away, squinting in the unfamiliar brightness. It seemed like a gust of air blew in, wafting their faces with a refreshing coolness. Echoing voices hailed them urgently from the other side.

'Stand clear. We'll be through in a couple of minutes. Hold on.'

The atmosphere was misty with the

disturbance of the landslide, dust rising to choke them once more, evoking a fit of coughing and spluttering but the discomfort was nothing compared with their elation. They would soon be free.

At last the barrier gave way to reveal what looked like a night sky peppered with stars as the safety lights of their rescuers tumbled down the remaining heap to kneel before them, shaking hands and patting them on the shoulder with words of encouragement and comfort.

'We'll soon have you out of here . . . '

'A nice cup of tea's waiting . . . '

Carol felt the tears trickling down her cheeks, realising they were safe at last and she'd soon see the grass and the sky. She could barely wait. After a quick examination of their arms and legs to ensure there were no broken bones, expert hands dragged them to their feet and they were half carried out of the tunnel where a bustling scene of activity greeted them.

The tranquillity they had found here

earlier was now shattered by the triumphant cries of a gang of yellow-coated rescuers, their hard hats gleaming almost white in the brilliant sunshine. An ambulance stood nearby and its crew hurried to their aid with emergency kits and breathing apparatus. A police car, its lights flashing, stood a little way off while two officers made notes in their pocket books before walking purposefully towards them.

'Thank your lucky stars the other young chap had the good sense to stay out of the shaft otherwise you might never have been found,' one of their rescuers said as he pressed a hot drink in Carol's hand.

Someone wrapped a blanket around her shoulders and the combined warmth suddenly comforted her as she squinted in the sunshine, an over-poweringly brilliant contrast after the darkness they had endured for so long. To her dismay, she felt great tears of relief trickling down her cheeks and she was loath to meet the eyes of the rescue team, knowing how foolish she and Mark had been, entering the mine tunnel. Seth had warned them it was dangerous but they had ignored his protests. Where was he?

She sniffed away the tears and dabbed her eyes on a corner of the blanket before looking around. Nearby, Mark, too, was being cosseted by a huddle of rescuers and he looked up, smiling weakly when he caught her eye. His face was a blur of dirt, his eyes starkly prominent in the mask of dust. She realised she must look the same and a surge of embarrassment caused the colour to rise, emphasising the awareness of her foolhardiness.

The two policemen were making more notes as they questioned a man. It was Seth! He was beside them but he seemed anxious to leave, noticeably edging away as they spoke. Then suddenly he was at her side, an arm draped round her shoulder, his fingers pressing into her arm.

'Thank God you're all right,' he said

over and over again, kissing the top of her head, her brow, her cheeks.

She melted into his arms, waiting for him to say, I told you so, and was relieved that he did not. Instead, he pulled a handkerchief from his pocket and with tender, gentle strokes, wiped her eyes and cheeks.

'You're all right now. Quite safe,' he said. 'So am I. I thought I'd burst my lungs running along the road to the museum to get them to phone for help. It seemed to take the crew ages to arrive but I suppose it was only a few minutes. I was halfway down the road on my way back here when they picked me up.'

'The car,' Carol said, with the memory of Mark's words troubling her. 'Why didn't you take the car.'

'Can't drive,' he said ruefully. 'Never learned and anyway, I noticed Mark shoving the keys in his pocket when we got here.'

The tension eased miraculously, instantly replaced by Carol's feelings of resentment when she remembered Mark's crazy accusations. She knew Seth would go for help. She did . . . Why was she trying to convince herself?

Everyone was moving now. The ambulance crew, satisfied that there were no casualties, backed their vehicle on to the road and drove off. The police car followed soon afterwards after Carol and Mark had given the officers a brief statement and received a polite, though firm admonishment regarding their unwise action of entering the mine. Mark stood, rather shamefacedly, looking at Seth.

'Thanks,' he said in a flat tone that betrayed his insincerity. 'Good thing you got those guys to dig us out.'

He nodded to the car.

'Let's get out of here. I'm ready for a hot tub. Looks like that should be one of your priorities, too, Carol.'

Wordlessly they followed him to the car and got in. Seth ushered Carol into the back seat and with his arm around her shoulder, steadied her on the journey until Mark drew to a halt outside the Traveller's Ease.

'I have to park this around back,' he called through the open window as they got out, then he drove off with an indifferent wave.

'His attitude is damned casual,' Seth said, frowning at the car disappearing around the corner. 'Considering it was his idea to go into the mine, I think he should be ashamed of himself. He could have got you both killed.'

Hanging his head, he traced small circles on the footpath with the toe of his shoe.

'I'm really cut up about suggesting we went there in the first place. I suppose it was all my fault.'

He was frowning as he raised his head to meet Carol's eyes.

'No one knew it would turn out like that,' she said, squeezing his arm. 'Anyway, none of us will do anything so foolish again, that's for sure. I know I've learned my lesson.'

She tried to reassure him with the words, relieved when at last he smiled. Carol noticed that passersby were casting curious glances in her direction and was instantly aware of how dishevelled and dirty she must look.

'I'll have to go and clean up.'

She grinned.

'It'll take me hours,' she said ruefully, brushing the dirt from her clothes.

'Will I see you later?'

She nodded, looking into his eyes and hoping she had not betrayed her earlier doubts about his honesty. He hadn't struck up a friendship because she might inherit the shop, and whatever else was listed in the Morrissey estate. She convinced herself, she did trust him. How could she love someone and not trust him?

At last in the comfortable privacy and security of her room, she flopped on to the bed and suddenly sobbed bitterly as Mark's words rose to taunt her.

He knows you're in line for a share of

the loot. Could be his interest's simply mercenary.

She glanced in the mirror and winced at the reflection. The tear-stained face, streaked with dirt and the limp hair, dulled and matted with dust, could never be considered attractive enough to make any young man declare his love. Even cleaned up she considered herself no beauty. How could she believe, even for a minute, that Seth had meant what he said?

For the first time since she arrived, she was homesick, for her own snug apartment, for Julie, even for the monotonous life she led. At that moment it seemed like a haven in a storm and she fervently wished she had never come to Falmouth and never heard of the Morrissey estate, Mark Hambel, and Seth Coombes.

9

Carol was surprised when there was no sign of Mark at dinner. His place setting had not been disturbed and even the waiter raised his eyes at her enquiry, acknowledging the empty chair. She was ravenous. Apart from the chewing gum Mark had given her and the hot drink from the rescue man, nothing had passed her lips since breakfast and the gnawing pains in her stomach reminded her of that fact.

Settling the napkin on her knee, she ate with a vengeance, occasionally glancing at the door to the restaurant as she waited for Mark to make a tardy entrance.

Satisfyingly replete, she sipped her coffee, suspecting that Mark would not come now. Perhaps he was suffering some ill effects from their imprisonment and she wondered if she should send a message to his room, or, better still, go and knock at his door to see if he was all right.

Folding her napkin and pushing back her chair, she made for the door. She would go to his room, believing it to be a friendly gesture though her feelings towards him were not so amicable. The number of his room was on the dining room table, propped up against the tiny vase of flowers, along with her own.

She walked up the stairs to the next landing, counting the door numbers until she came to the one she sought. There were sounds of activity inside, someone moving around and the noise of furniture being shifted. Tapping softly, she waited. The door was opened by a maid, fresh linen in her hand and her eyes saucer like with surprise.

'Sorry, miss, I thought you was the gentleman coming back for something you'd forgotten. Visitors often do after they've checked out,' she said brightly.

Carol's mouth drooped and the maid

hastened to add, 'Is there anything I can do for you, miss?'

'Er . . . no . . . thank you.'

Carol backed away and took the lift to the foyer where she was told that the young American gentleman, Mr Hambel, had vacated his room just before dinner this evening and as far as they knew, had left to travel to London. And no, sorry, he had not given them any intimation that he would be returning.

Carol was stunned. Apart from being such an unusual thing to do, to leave the Morrissey legacy hanging in the balance, she wondered what reason had prompted Mark to leave so abruptly without even saying goodbye.

His interest in the Morrissey estate had far surpassed her own. He had seemed to be taking it all far more seriously than she was. It was strange that he should leave his claim in the hands of Mr Dodson, the solicitor, when it seemed that all would be decided in a few days. There was something decidedly odd here, she thought.

Carol shrugged and went out into the street, her mind a riot of conflicting thoughts. Outside, she was buffeted from all sides, running the gauntlet of holidaymakers, as she sidled along the narrow footpath and down to the quayside pub where she and Seth usually met. He was waiting at one of the outside tables and jumped up to greet her.

'No hangovers,' he asked, looking her over, 'from this afternoon? Are you all right?'

Carol flopped on to a chair and nodded, forcing a smile.

'You'll never guess,' she began. 'Mark has checked out of the hotel and gone back to London. They told me at Reception that as far as they know, he's not coming back.'

'Best thing he could do in the circumstances.'

He frowned with an air of indignation.

'Maybe he's realised what an idiot he was this afternoon and he's too embarrassed to face you. Quite right, too.'

'But what about the business with the solicitor?' Carol asked. 'I'm surprised he's left all that in the balance when it should be decided in a few days, and anyway, it wouldn't have cost him anything to say goodbye. Just downright rude, I think. I really thought he would have stayed on to make sure his interests were being well represented by Mr Dodson. After all he had to say about . . .'

She hesitated, realising she was rambling on almost incoherently. She was aware of Seth's eyes on her as he waited for her to go on. She turned away, anxious to veer the conversation in another direction but Seth was not so easily deterred.

'All he had to say about what?' he prompted.

Carol took a deep breath, realising that she could no longer evade the issue.

'He said he thought you were only interested in me because I might inherit the shop, and that you really resented the two of us for getting in your way, that you'd get rid of us if you could.'

Seth's face hardened and an angry flush crept up his neck.

'And what about you?' he asked. 'Is that what you think, too? That's the kind of man you think I am?'

The harsh tone of his voice rose and she hesitated, carefully selecting the words with which to answer him but the pause was long enough to enrage him still further. He sprang up and pushed away his chair.

'Seems like there's nothing else to be said then,' he said in a voice like splintering glass. 'I'll be off now. I'm sure you don't want me hanging around any longer when you have such a low opinion of me. After all, there's a chance I might poison you by slipping a few pills in your glass,' he added with a snarl that contorted his face.

With that, he spun on his heel and

stomped away, hands thrust in his pockets and his back bent as if carrying the cares of the world on his shoulders as he trudged away up the hill. He turned a corner and was lost from sight.

With a sinking heart, Carol watched him go. She was drained of emotion. Too much had happened today. She had offended Seth by repeating Mark's accusations and if she was truly honest, she must admit, that she, too, had wondered about his real interest in her. Pangs of remorse tore at the pit of her stomach, realising she was as guilty as Mark for doubting him.

For a moment she sat looking down at the harbour, watching reflections of the strings of flickering coloured lights break into a thousand fragments, dappling the inky blackness with a moving patchwork of colour. But its beauty went unregistered as her heart lurched in its emptiness. She was determined that she, like Mark, would go back to London where the memories of Falmouth would be buried. She knew she had hurt Seth terribly and he had made it clear he never wanted to see her again.

★ ★ ★

In a fug of self remorse, she trudged along the street to the hotel. Once back at the Traveller's Ease, she began to throw her clothes into the suitcase, making plans for the following day. Unlike Mark, she would inform Mr Dodson of her plans.

An excuse for the hasty departure could be easily concocted. After all, she reasoned, his letter had found her before. It could just as easily find her again should he have news of the legacy.

As it happened, Mr Dodson contacted her by telephone, the following morning, as she was entering the dining room. His usually buoyant voice seemed strangely muted and spiritless as he invited her to his office at a mutually agreed time.

'I look forward to seeing you,' he'd said but the flat tone insinuated otherwise.

Carol arrived promptly at Welwyn, Carter and Dodson where she was told Mr Dodson was expecting her and she was immediately shown into his office. The vertical blinds were closed today and the room was in a comparative gloom that cast the solicitor's face into shadow.

'Ah! How good to see you, Miss Trevallan. Do sit down,' he greeted her formally.

He indicated a chair and Carol perched nervously on the edge waiting for him to broach the reason for his urgent summons.

'I have now to hand all the details of this rather messy search to find the rightful heir to the Morrissey estate. You do realise, I hope, that although we instigated the enquiries, we are not responsible for what they have unearthed. Their findings are quite out of our control and our company may only act for the rightful heir.'

Carol wished he would get on with it but the man seemed to like the sound of his own voice.

'No doubt you are aware that Mr Hambel has left for London.'

He paused giving Carol time to nod, her eyes widening at the fact that he knew.

'I spoke to him late yesterday afternoon with the details. Incidentally, I understand you both had a lucky escape at that disused mine. Very unfortunate business. Could have been tragic so he tells me. I'm surprised that young Coombes invited you inside.'

Carol wanted to protest that it hadn't been like that, but she remained silent, willing him to resume the discussion about the estate.

'Should have been fenced off, out of bounds years ago. No doubt this little escapade will ensure that it is made safe now.'

He leaned back in the leather chair and his mouth curled in a smile.

'Now, where was I? Ah, yes! We have at last ascertained to whom the estate should be bequeathed.'

He paused and ruffled the papers on his desk, peering at her over the rim of his spectacles.

'We have determined the true heir.'

Before he could continue, Carol said quietly, 'Mark . . . Mr Hambel suggested that whichever one of us should inherit the estate, we would divide it equally between the two of us. No doubt he told you when you spoke to him. He said that was the fairer way of doing things.'

She shrugged.

'It was his idea. He seemed to have strong views, and I agreed.'

She shrugged again, feeling totally inadequate and rather embarrassed to have interrupted the solicitor who was regarding her bemusedly. Hanging her head, she remained silent now, willing him to go on. When he, too, remained silent, she looked up to find his plump face lined with concern.

'My dear young lady,' he began, 'I informed Mr Hambel last night that it has emerged that the bulk of the estate will pass to him as it has been ascertained that he is the rightful heir. He gave me no instructions regarding the arrangements that you have just mentioned.'

For a moment they looked at one another then Mr Dodson spoke.

'I agree that the action you mentioned would have been far more fitting, in my humble estimation, but the executors have decreed that there is one rightful heir and one must abide by their decision. It is most unfortunate that Mr Hambel gave me no instructions regarding your inclusion considering the suggestion he made.'

He pressed his fingertips together and beat a silent tattoo in his familiar mannerism as he stared across the desk.

'I have no doubt that you would have honoured this gentleman's agreement should the matter of the estate have been reversed. However, it seems that our Mr Hambel might have forgotten the suggestion he made,' he said matter-of-factly.

There was a slight curl to his lips as he said the latter and Carol reasoned that he, like herself, was sceptical about Mark's denial.

'Leave it with me, Miss Trevallan. I will contact the American gentleman and make further enquiries before I contact you again at the Traveller's. Incidentally, I hope you have enough money to meet your immediate needs. Naturally, you will not lose out financially on any expenses incurred. I'll see that you are fully reimbursed. The estate can well afford that much,' he said, frowning as he scribbled on a pad lying on the desk.

Despite Carol's protests, he insisted that he would be in touch with Mr Hambel and ushered her from his office with a protective arm around her shoulder rather than the more usual curt handshake. Carol sensed that she had found an ally and the thought cheered her, lightening the cloud of depression that enveloped her when she remembered she had been deceived by Mark and deserted by Seth.

Unfortunately, she must now stay on in Falmouth, at least for another day. It would be rude and ungrateful for her to leave when Mr Dodson had shown so much concern for her well-being. Ah, well, she sighed, another day won't make that much difference.

Back at the hotel, she emptied her suitcase and hung up her things in a haphazard fashion, feeling numbed, lost and bewildered, wondering how she could pass away the time until it would be opportune for her to leave.

Wandering aimlessly through the streets, Carol found herself outside The Treasure Chest and pressed her brow to the glass to look inside, half hoping that Seth was engaged in his regular task of cleaning up. But no tell-tale light burned at the rear of the shop.

The dim interior was lost in shadow and she noticed a film of dust on the display of goods in the window. Before long everything would be thrown away, all the stock that Seth's uncle had amassed over the years, the fisherman's weights adorning the ceiling, the boxes of buckets and spades and with them all of Seth's dreams for the future.

The thoughts troubled her as she gazed inside, oblivious to others jostling by on the footpath. Sadly, she turned away, knowing that life would have been simpler had she never stumbled across the old shop and had never met Seth Coombes.

He was never far away in her thoughts and she was uncomfortable about the way they had parted, guilty to have misjudged his motives and feeling decidedly foolish to have voiced them aloud.

As if in a daze, she wandered down to the quay where the last of the trawlers was being unloaded. Seth's boat was securely anchored and appeared to be deserted. No doubt he would be at home after his day's work.

She turned away but an insistent tug on her arm had her turning to meet the twinkling eyes of a seaman with weathered brown skin, crinkled like ancient parchment.

'You be looking for Seth? I've seen you here before.'

She nodded, looking around, expecting . . . hoping . . . for him to suddenly appear.

'He's gone to Truro. Hopes to sign on with a salvage crew. Better money than we gets hereabouts even though it means packing up and living out of a duffle bag.'

He grinned.

'Good life for a man with no ties.'

He nodded, his face breaking into a graph of lines when a smile wrinkled the corners of his mouth.

Raising a finger to his brow in the semblance of a salute, he moved away to hoist a creel of fish farther along the quay.

Carol's heart sank into the pit of her stomach. So Seth, too, was leaving without saying goodbye. What was it about her, she wondered, that provoked people to remove themselves from her life, whatever the reason. Her mother and father, Aunt Maisie, Mark Hambel and now Seth.

It was the last name that bothered her most and hot tears of self pity, mingled with anger and frustration, battled behind her eyelids.

10

Back at the Traveller's Ease, she wrote Seth a brief note, intending to walk up the hill to his cottage and push it through the letterbox. She'd feel better if she made some attempt to redeem herself in his eyes, though she knew it was unlikely they would ever meet again. At least she could tell him of the outcome of the Morrissey estate, that Mark Hambel was Uncle Jim's nearest relation.

How strange it had all turned out, she thought as she screwed up one sheet of paper after another in a faltering attempt to express her feelings in words.

Finally, half satisfied with what she had written, sealing the envelope, she shoved it in her pocket and left the room, with a heavy heart. In the foyer, when she emerged from the lift, the receptionist called her name and pointed to a figure standing in the doorway.

'There's someone inquiring for you, Miss Trevallan. I was just about to ring your room.'

It was Seth and he turned to look at her, his face brightening as she approached.

'I'm sorry that . . . '

'I was just going . . . '

They spoke together and then stopped, the event causing a smile to lighten the situation. Seth took advantage of the lull between them to voice an apology.

'I had no right to speak to you like I did. You were just telling me what the American said. They weren't your words and I should have realised that. I was hurt and I've been angry with myself ever since for walking away. I was too stupid and proud to come back, until now.'

He reached for her hand and she met his halfway, her own words tumbling

144

over as her heart filled with renewed joy at seeing him again.

'*I almost believed him,*' *she said quietly.* '*What he implied made me feel* so ugly and undesirable. I know I'm nothing special. I really wondered why you chose to spend so much time with me. Mark convinced me that it was only the fact I might get all that money that had attracted you to me in the first place.'

Seth's arms went round her instantly and he would have kissed her had they both not noticed they were being well and truly scrutinised by the receptionist who noticeably cocked her ears to catch their every word.

'Let's get out of here,' he whispered, his face breaking into a smile as wide as her own. 'Let's find somewhere we can talk.'

The letter in Carol's pocket rustled as they sat down at the quayside bar and she pulled it out, pushing it across the table to him. With a puzzled expression he picked it up, turning it over and over before she urged him to read it.

'It was difficult to write,' she said quietly, 'but it tells you how I feel. It would be a shame if you didn't read it after all the struggle I had to get it down.'

He tore open the envelope and his eyes quickly scanned the single page. When he finished, he folded the letter and slowly replaced it in the envelope, his face a mixture of expressions that Carol could not decipher.

'So,' he said at last, 'it looks like that rogue walks off with all uncle's possessions. I hadn't realised there was more at stake than the shop. I fancy Uncle Jim never knew that there was money in the background. Might have changed his life if he had. He could have bought himself a little comfort in his old age.'

His eyes grew distant and he hung his head. Carol sensed that tears were not far away as he murmured, 'Poor Uncle Jim.'

146

Eventually he looked up and smiled, reaching for her hand.

'I'm sorry, love, that you've missed out on everything. Your luck is as bad as mine. But there's an old saying — what you've never had, you never miss. We both know what that means.'

Carol raised her shoulders.

'I guessed all along it had nothing to do with me. Legacies don't fall like apples in front of people like me.'

'You being so dull and ordinary,' he added, echoing her words of a minute ago with a broad smile.

He bent over to snatch her hand from where it lay on the chequered tablecloth.

'I hope this doesn't meant that you intend leaving.'

His face was suddenly tense and he gripped her fingers so tightly they smarted in his fist.

'Don't go, Carol. Stay here and marry me. I love you.'

Her heart rose with joy, then as suddenly plummeted like a diving bird.

'But you're going away, too,' she said falteringly. 'A man at the quay told me you'd gone to sign up on a salvage crew.'

'Only if you turn me down. I was coming here first to ask you to marry me.'

He hesitated as the words she'd spoken seemed to register with their full implication.

'You went looking for me on the quay?'

'I couldn't leave it like this.'

'Because you love me, too? Say it, Carol. Tell me you love me,' he asked, his voice filled with anxiety.

She nodded, meeting his eyes with her own, awash with tears that tumbled down her cheeks.

'Yes,' she said quietly. 'I do.'

'Then that's all we need, our love for each other. You can move into the cottage right away and we'll get married just as soon as I can make the arrangements.'

He sprang from the chair and

dragged her to her feet, clasping his arms around her in a fierce hug that had her gasping for breath. Waltzing a couple of steps, he put her down and dropped to his knee before her on the pavement.

'Remember, a few days ago I promised I'd do this properly?' he said, a twinkle in his eyes.

Carol nodded, laughing through the tears as she tried to tug him to his feet.

'People are looking at us,' she muttered. 'Get up.'

Seth ignored her pleas and continued, 'Carol! Will you marry me?'

'Yes!' she whispered. 'Yes, get up.'

As he rose to his feet, a trickle of applause erupted from others seated nearby, their faces beaming at the spectacle they had just witnessed. Someone sent a bottle of wine to their table and everyone cheered enthusiastically as eventually Seth kissed his new fiancée.

★   ★   ★

Walking back to the hotel, he squeezed her fingers.

'Pack your case and I'll wait. I'll carry it up to the cottage now. You can move in straightaway. I'm afraid to let you out of my sight again in case I lose you.'

Carol hesitated.

'I'm not sure that's a good idea. I want to do this properly. I don't mean a flashy white wedding and all that, but . . . '

The words tumbled over as she struggled to explain.

'It's all too sudden.'

'That sounds just like a line of dialogue from a second rate movie.'

Seth laughed as she fell silent for a few moments.

'I . . . I want to enjoy being engaged to you, only for a few days,' she said eventually, in whispered tones. 'My room is booked at the hotel until the end of the week.'

'Ah, now I understand.'

He grinned.

'You don't want to miss out on all this luxury to come and live with me in a hovel.'

She gasped with indignation.

'Your cottage isn't a hovel. It's the most beautiful house I've ever seen.'

'And we're going to be very happy there.'

Seth was no longer laughing as he wrapped his arms around her, drawing Carol to him as he traced soft gentle kisses on her cheeks and eyelids.

'People are looking,' Carol said, conscious of the interested glances of passersby. 'And you're not listening.'

Holding her at arms' length he nodded.

'I'm listening. While you're staying here I'll make all the arrangements for the wedding. As soon as possible?' he asked.

Carol was unable to answer for the joy that rose in her throat to engulf her with happiness.

She nodded, whispering, 'As soon as possible.'

11

Seth was true to his word and the marriage plans were arranged swiftly with the help of a special licence. The wedding was to be on the Saturday afternoon that Carol vacated her room at the Traveller's Ease. Crosslegged on her bed, she sat quietly one evening and wrote to Julia telling her the good news and enclosing a letter of resignation to the office.

Julie replied without delay, profuse in her good wishes and regretting the fact that she could not be at the wedding.

Do be sure about what you're doing, she wrote. *After all, if he's a sailor he may have a wife in every port. I'd hate to think of you as being number three or four in line. There's lots of strange stories about sailors. I really miss you. Incidentally, when I go to the park at lunchtimes now, I swear the ducks are looking for you. They seem to be waiting for something all the time.*

Carol chuckled as she read the letter which served to brighten her spirits still further as the wedding day drew nearer.

On the afternoon before, she packed her case in readiness for Seth to move to his cottage at the top of the hill and in her euphoria told the receptionist she was getting married the following day.

'Hadn't you better inform Mr Dodson?' she asked. 'If he leaves any messages for you and you're not here . . .'

The words trailed off, instigating Carol to make a telephone call to the offices of Welwyn, Carter and Dodson.

'Congratulations!' the resonant voice of Mr Dodson boomed. 'This is good news indeed. So your visit to Falmouth has paid dividends after all.'

He chuckled.

'You've found yourself a husband, a true Cornishman at that. Incidentally,' he went on in a less ebullient tone, 'I've spoken to our mutual friend, Mr Mark

Hambel, and he states, most emphatically, that he has no remembrance of the . . . as it were . . . gentleman's agreement you mentioned. There appears to be a decided block on the issue. Unfortunate, but there it is. I understand he will be returning to the States in the next few days so any future business will be by letter.'

He sighed noisily.

'However, your forthcoming marriage surmounts any disappointment you may have had regarding the Morrissey estate. I'm sure we both wish the young man joy with his inheritance.'

His resigned voice betrayed little enthusiasm for the sentiments he had voiced leaving Carol in no doubt that Mr Dodson had little regard for Mark Hambel.

Carol shrugged as she replaced the receiver. She had not been surprised that Mark had reneged on the arrangement he had been quick to introduce when it appeared he might lose out on the inheritance. He was welcome to it, she thought. I have Seth.

Saturday's sunshine seemed brighter than any other day since she came to Falmouth, Carol thought, pulling the curtains aside and gazing into the clear blue sky. And today is my wedding day! A medley of emotions tormented her as she wondered what her parents would have thought of Seth.

And dear Aunt Maisie, how she would miss her being at the church, too. Her isolation pressed in to engulf her in a web of self pity until she realised, from today onwards, she would never have to be alone again. There would be Seth.

A veritable army of butterflies invaded her stomach as she went into the dining room for breakfast, their wings fluttering so incessantly that she knew she would never be able to eat a thing. Glancing at her watch she counted the hours to the ceremony, wondering how she would survive until then.

Nursing a cup of coffee, she gazed

into space, anticipating the excitement of the day ahead, when someone coughed politely to attract her attention. The reverie shattered, she looked up to see the waitresses massed in a circle around her table. One blushed furiously as she withdrew her arm, previously hidden behind her back.

'This is for you,' she said shyly, 'compliments of the management.'

She held out a bridal bouquet of red roses, resplendent with trailing fern and spiralling red ribbons, while the others smiled, offering a chorus of good wishes. Carol gasped, the tears rushing to her eyes. She was unable to speak and sat numbly at the table until another waitress stepped forward pressing a weighty package into her hand.

'A little wedding gift from the girls.'

She giggled.

'Representing the joys and the tears of marriage. Go on!' she urged. 'Open it!'

The others surged forward, crowding round the table as Carol fumbled with the wrapping paper. Inside was a large bag of sugar and a packet of salt. She began to smile through the tears that coursed down her cheeks, surprised when yet another two of the waitresses set more packages on the table.

'Something to flavour the tears.'

They grinned, as Carol unwrapped a bottle of vinegar.

'And something to heighten the joys,' the other said, looking pleased when to her delight, Carol discovered a huge bottle of champagne.

She mumbled her gratitude, dabbing her eyes with the napkin.

'You are all so kind,' she said, knowing how inadequate were her words for the friendly gestures that had tugged unmercilessly at her heart.

But it was not over yet, as she discovered when the girls went on to tell her that a wedding cake had been delivered to the cottage, another gift from the staff. Carol proudly carried the strange assortment of presents to her room and packed them away to be taken to her new home, her heart glowing as the wedding hour approached.

* ★ ★ ★

Seth called at the hotel to take Carol to church, proudly leading her along the street, carrying her bridal bouquet. To their surprise, on the steps of the tiny church, stood a beaming Mr Dodson, complete with a white carnation buttonhole. His spectacles gleamed in the sunshine but did not hide the wide smile he beamed as they drew nearer.

'I hope you don't mind this intrusion on your nuptials,' he said, 'but I couldn't let this happy occasion go by unnoticed. May I have the honour?'

He proffered his arm and Carol instinctively allowed him to escort her inside.

'Go along, Coombes, there's a good chap,' he whispered hoarsely. 'Shouldn't you be waiting at the altar or something?'

He gave Seth a gentle push sending him hurrying to the front of the church where, after a few minutes, the minister appeared from the vestry.

'No second thoughts?' Mr Dodson whispered in a fatherly tone. 'Now's the time, young lady. In a few minutes it will be too late.'

Not expecting a reply, with the carriage of a king, he led Carol along the aisle to where her bridegroom waited.

Back outside the church, Mr Dodson shook hands with Seth, congratulating him on his choice of a bride but as Carol proffered her hand, he pushed it aside.

'My privilege, I think,' he said, bending to kiss her cheek.

Fumbling in his pocket he withdrew two envelopes and handed them to Carol, smiling at Seth as he did so.

'I'm sure the new Mrs Coombes will acquaint you of their contents in due course. And now I'm afraid I have to leave you two newly-weds to your fate,' he said, sounding, to Carol, a trifle mysterious.

With a friendly wave he disappeared into the crowd of holidaymakers meandering along the street, eyeing the newly weds with undisguised interest. Seth tugged Carol into the secure harbour made by one of the church buttresses and gathered her into his arms.

'Old Dodson has kissed the bride,' he whispered, 'but I haven't.'

With that, his eager mouth stopped Carol's protest that everyone was watching them and she succumbed to the wishes of her new husband.

12

Seth filled cardboard boxes with discarded goods that they'd agreed they would never sell and stacked them in a line by the front door of The Treasure Chest. Carol hummed softly, sprinkling water on the shop floor before she swept away several weeks' accumulated dust lying in layers on the ancient linoleum.

'I'm glad we're keeping the old name, The Treasure Chest,' she said. 'It's full of mystery and imagination. I rather like it. It would be impossible to come up with a better name for a place like this.'

'Yes, me, too. I'm not sure who called it that originally. The shop's been called The Treasure Chest for as long as I can remember.'

He set a box down on the floor and lolled against the counter looking at her.

'Who would have thought it,' he said grinning, 'that the inquisitive woman who wandered in here by mistake should end up as my wife?'

'Are you sorry?' Carol asked provocatively, glancing at him coyly from beneath half-lowered eyelids.

'Well, I was hoping for a bigger share but I'll settle for what I've got.'

He ducked, chuckling and squirming when Carol threw a grubby duster at his head.

'We've been very lucky,' he said, serious now as he walked the few yards between them. 'Who would have thought that miserable American, Mark Hambel, would've had second thoughts about sharing things with you, even if it was only the shop he handed over. I suppose it was too much bother going through all the business of negotiating a sale, so he just took what ready cash there was from the tin mine investment and ran.'

His lip curled in contempt.

'Getting the shop was thanks to Mr

Dodson,' Carol reminded him. 'I think he made Mark feel like a perfect heel for what he did, skipping out of town as soon as he got to know everything went to him. Imagine denying that he'd got me to promise to share it all if the estate came my way. He obviously didn't want to face me.'

She flicked the duster along the counter as if pushing aside the unhappy memory.

'Not that I would have held him to the bargain anyway. I never really expected anything. Always felt that someone had made a mistake bringing me into it. I certainly never thought we'd end up with The Treasure Chest, with all this.'

She looked around as she had done the first time she set foot in the shop, her eyes thrilling to the strange variety of goods lining the walls, hanging from the ceiling and stacked in boxes and wicker baskets on the floor.

'Neither did I,' Seth said but it was

Carol he was looking at as he pulled her into his arms. 'We'll try to make a go of the shop, give it a chance and who knows, maybe it will be a treasure chest for us.'

'And our son,' Carol whispered.

'Mmm.'

Seth's kiss came suddenly to an end.

'Our son?' he said quizzically, holding her at arms' length to peer into her face.

'Or daughter, whatever we have.'

'Oh, my love,' he murmured. 'What more can life hold for us?'

'Not very much if we don't get on with the work,' Carol suggested practically, easing away from the enclosure of his arms. 'There's lots to do if we want to be open for next summer's trade. And the signwriter will be here soon, so let's get busy.'

'Are you sure that's what we should do with Mr Dodson's cheque?' he asked.

'We agreed.'

Carol smiled.

'The wedding present was for both of us and it seems right we should have the old sign outside freshened up. This is where we met. It will always be special for me.'

Her eyes were suddenly misty as she hurried into the stock room at the rear. A few minutes later she called to Seth, popping her head around the open door.

'What about all these boxes of buckets and spades and these old postcards?' she asked, pushing a stray lock of hair from her forehead.

He leaned against the door post, frowning.

'Maybe we can offload them on to one of the tourist shops. If we sell them cheaply, they can make a good profit on the deal. I'll ask around. As for the postcards, how many boxes?'

He counted, prodding them with a finger.

'Four altogether. Probably those old saucy ones that nobody seems to buy these days.'

He drew a hand through his hair.

'I don't suppose anyone will want them. We'll just have to put them out for scrap.'

He carried a box into the shop and laid it on the counter, laughing at Carol who followed him.

'Some of those postcards were considered to be quite rude in their day. Do you remember? All ladies with big bosoms and captions that were intended to have double meanings.'

Carol grinned.

'Aunt Maisie used to be so embarrassed if one dropped on her doormat. Anyone would have thought she'd sent it herself. 'Whatever will the postman think,' she used to say. Shall we look at some of them before we throw them away?'

Seth prised the top from one of the boxes, and opened the brown paper enclosure.

'They really protected their goods a few years ago,' he said. 'Not like today when everything's stuck up with sticky tape and rubbery glue and packed in polystyrene.'

Carol helped to turn back the brown paper and they both stood silently, studying the contents of the box.

'These aren't saucy postcards,' she whispered, touching one with a tentative finger tip. 'Look at the lace and ribbons on them.'

'They're postcards all right,' Seth said in a voice as hushed as hers. 'But much older than the ones we were talking about.'

Without exploring further, he covered the box and hurried into the stock room returning after a moment carrying the other three. On inspection, these, too, contained a variety of delicately-trimmed, ornate postcards of a bygone age, some intended for birthdays and anniversaries. The last one was filled with nothing but Christmas cards.

'These boxes must have been here nearly a hundred years. I'm no expert but even an idiot knows, no one's made this kind of thing for a long time.'

'That could make them valuable,' Carol said quietly, selecting a card from one of the boxes and running her fingers over the delicately ruched lace trimmings.

'Valuable, yes.'

13

Seth raised his head slowly to look at her, his eyes burning with the exultant fire of discovery.

'Collectors would pay a fortune for these. They're in mint condition,' he said excitedly.

He grabbed Carol by the waist and hoisted her from her feet giving an animal-like roar as he set her down again.

'Darling, do you know what this means? We can afford to buy in some new stock. I can go round the antique fairs and pick up a few bargains.'

'You hope!'

'And we'll still have enough left to get the alterations made to the shop, the plans we talked about, remember?'

Seth's excitement was contagious and Carol found herself laughing uncontrollably as she flung her arms around his neck. Remembering something he'd said when they first met, she was immediately sober, cupping his face with her hands and holding him away when he tried to kiss her.

'Seth! Listen! Didn't you say there was a whole jumble of old stock upstairs?'

His eyes widened.

'That's right!'

For a moment they were silent, staring at one another, each speculating on what treasures they might find secreted away upstairs.

'Well! Seems like this is a real treasure chest. What do you say?' he was asking.

Carol was quiet, unable to control the tears of joy that fled in rivulets down her cheeks.

Swallowing with difficulty, she gasped, 'What do I say? I say thank you, Uncle Jim, for looking after us.'

For a moment they clung together, poring over the sentiment until at last Seth whispered in her ear, 'Do you suppose he's watching us right now?'

Carol looked over his shoulder and her eyes misted as she took in the shop at a glance.

'He'll always be here, in our hearts.'

THE END

We do hope that you have enjoyed reading this large print book.

Did you know that all of our titles are available for purchase?

We publish a wide range of high quality large print books including:
Romances, Mysteries, Classics
General Fiction
Non Fiction and Westerns

Special interest titles available in large print are:
The Little Oxford Dictionary
Music Book, Song Book
Hymn Book, Service Book

Also available from us courtesy of Oxford University Press:
Young Readers' Dictionary
(large print edition)
Young Readers' Thesaurus
(large print edition)

For further information or a free brochure, please contact us at:
Ulverscroft Large Print Books Ltd.,
The Green, Bradgate Road, Anstey,
Leicester, LE7 7FU, England.
Tel: (00 44) **0116 236 4325**
Fax: (00 44) **0116 234 0205**

SUMMER IN HANOVER SQUARE

Charlotte Grey

The impoverished Margaret Lambart is suddenly flung into all the glitter of the Season in Regency London. Suspected by her godmother's nephew, the influential Marquis St. George, of being merely a common adventuress, she has, nevertheless, a brilliant success, and attracts the attentions of the young Duke of Oxford. However, when the Marquis discovers that Margaret is far from wanting a husband he finds he has to revise his estimate of her true worth.

CONFLICT OF HEARTS

Gillian Kaye

Somerset, at the end of World War I: Daniel Holley, unhappily married to an ailing wife and father of four grown-up children, is attracted to beautiful schoolteacher Harriet Bray, but he knows his love is hopeless. Daniel's only daughter, Amy, who dreams of becoming a milliner and is caught up in her love for young bank clerk John Tottle, looks on as the drama of Daniel and Harriet's fate and happiness gradually unfolds.

THE SOLDIER'S WOMAN

Freda M. Long

When Lieutenant Alain d'Albert was deserted by his girlfriend, a replacement was at hand in the shape of Christina Calvi, whose yearning for respectability through marriage did not quite coincide with her profession as a soldier's woman. Christina's obsessive love for Alain was not returned. The handsome hussar married an heiress and banished the soldier's woman from his life. But Christina was unswerving in the pursuit of her dream and Alain found his resistance weakening . . .

THE TENDER DECEPTION

Laura Rose

When Sophia Barton was taken from Curton Workhouse to be a scullery-maid at Perriman Court, her future looked bleak. Was it really an act of Providence that persuaded Lady Perriman to adopt her as her ward? Sophia was brought up together with the Perriman children, and before sailing with his regiment for India, George, the heir to the title, declared his love. But tragedy hit the family and Sophia found herself caught up in a web of mystery and intrigue.

CONVALESCENT HEART

Lynne Collins

They called Romily the Snow Queen, but once she had been all fire and passion, kindled into loving by a man's kiss and sure it would last a lifetime. She still believed it would, for her. It had lasted only a few months for the man who had stormed into her heart. After Greg, how could she trust any man again? So was it likely that surgeon Jake Conway could pierce the icy armour that the lovely ward sister had wrapped about her emotions?